The Price of Beauty in Strawberry Land

http://www.carsonrenomysteryseries.com

http://www.geraldwdarnell.com

The Price of Beauty in Strawberry Land

A Carson Reno Mystery

Gerald W. Darnell

cr press

ISBN 978-1-257-08529-3

Be sure to check out Carson Reno's other Mystery Adventures

Murder in Humboldt

The Price of Beauty in Strawberry Land

Killer Among Us

Horse Tales

SUnset 4

the Crossing

the Illegals

the Everglades

Dead Men Don't Remember

The Fingerprint Murders

Reelfoot

JUSTIFIABLE HOMICIDE

Dead End

Murder and More

DEADLY DECISION

SHADOWS & LIES

Murder my Darling

Cast of Characters

Carson Reno - Private Detective

Rita - Hostess Starlight Lounge

Marcie – Peabody Hotel Telephone Operator

Andy – Bartender at the *'Down Under'*

Nickie/Ronnie Woodson – Owners Chief's Motel and Restaurant

Tommy Trubush – carhop Chief's

Jack Logan – Attorney/Partner

Leroy Epsee – Sheriff Gibson County

Jeff Cole – Deputy Gibson County

Scotty Perry – Deputy Gibson County

Elizabeth Teague – Airline Stewardess and friend of Carson's

Mary Ellen Maxwell – Humboldt Socialite and owner of Maxwell Trucking

Judy Strong – Vice President of Maxwell Trucking

Gerald Wayne – Owner Wayne Knitting Mill

Nuddy – Bartender Humboldt Country Club

Dr. Barker - Coroner

Larry Parker – Chief of Detectives Shelby County

Brian Jeffers – Ex-Mayor of Memphis

Monica Jeffers – Wife of Brian Jeffers

Mason 'Booker-T' Brown – Head porter Peabody Hotel

Barry 'Butch' Lassiter – Chief Aide to Mayor

Darlene Lassiter – Wife of Barry Lassiter

Kathy Ledbetter – Employee Bosley Buick

Sam Ledbetter – Husband of Kathy Ledbetter

Charles/Carlon Bosley – Brothers and owners of Bosley Buick

Roger Thurbush – Mayor of Memphis

Susan Oakley – Mayor's political advisor

Randy Price – Mayor's bodyguard

Chuck Hutchinson – Memphis Police Chief

Carlton Scruggs – Shelby County Sheriff

Steve Carrollton – Head of Memphis Mafia

Bubba Knight – Mafia associate

Bobby James – Mafia associate

Watson Clark – Reporter Commercial Appeal

Amy Clark – Wife of Watson Clark

Amos Duncan – Father of Amy Clark

Bernie Taylor – Reporter Commercial Appeal

Alfred E. Dollar – Car thief

Brad Knuchols – Mafia associate

Jordan Bailey – Car salesman

Charlotte Luckey – Former Strawberry Hostess Princess

James 'Jimmy' Gannon – Football Coach

Barbara Stevens – ex-wife of James Gannon

Lee Stevens – Husband of Barbara Stevens

Loretta Turner – Charlotte Luckey's mother

Curtis Turner – Loretta Turner's husband/Charlotte's stepfather

Travis Luckey – Charlotte Luckey's father

Billy Vickers – Charlotte's ex-boyfriend

Mickey Campbell – Bookie and Mafia associate

Phillip Chaney – Memphis playboy and Charlotte's boyfriend

Denny Smith – Phillip's half brother

Forrest Chaney – Father of Phillip and Denny

Ted Blaylock – Manager Humboldt Airport

Tony Russoti – Mafia associate

Joe Brody – Mafia associate

Dedication

Our Teachers

Ewing Jackson and Theda Gee

Contribution Credits

Mary Ann Sizer Fisher

Elizabeth Tillman White

Judy Steele Minnehan

Material Credits

Humboldt Public Library

Gibson County Historical Website

Libby Lynch

www.carsonrenomysteryseries.com

The year is 1962 and Carson Reno, once again, gets himself into situations that would be better left alone. A Memphis client hires Carson to prove infidelity, but instead he finds corruption and murder going all the way to the top of Memphis politics.

A Jack Logan client investigation takes him back to Humboldt looking into automobile fraud, which lands him smack in the middle of a murder. Not just any murder, but the murder of a local beauty queen – one who seemed to have too many enemies for a girl her age.

Come along and find out what the real price of beauty is in...Strawberry Land

Chapters

Strawberry Festival Queen & Court 1963

"Life is cheap – make sure you buy enough".

®

Carson Reno

INTRODUCTION

*B*eauty – real beauty is both a curious and interesting thing.

Of course there are varying degrees of beauty, depending upon the beholder. But what is seen as beautiful to one is, more than likely, beautiful to everyone.

A beautiful woman will always retain her beauty. Regardless of age, wrinkles, even weight loss or gain – you can still see their magic and that thing we recognize as beauty. It's unexplainable, but the things that made them beautiful still remain.

Age can alter how our eyes define this beauty, but it doesn't remove that underlying image which made them what they had always been – beautiful.

Only death has the ability to change this image and rob the beauty that was once so easily recognizable. In normal death most remain as beautiful as they did in life. But, in violent death things are often different. The beauty dissolves and something horrific is inserted in its place. Those things we knew and recognized as beauty are gone – replaced by death and the circumstances of death. It erases everything.

~

*S*he had been in the water for more than 72 hours. Rigor mortis had come and gone, and her body had begun to bloat – like a dead floating fish. Little water animals had already started to nibble at her exposed body, leaving shreds of skin dangling for other predators to bite.

The corpse was never intended to be found, as is usually the case. This would have probably been accomplished, except for an ambitious fisherman.

~

*I*ke Murray knew the exact spot for he and his son, Rusty, to find fish in Humboldt Lake. A few yards back up in an unnoticed feeder creek is where Ike and Rusty had been catching their largemouth bass. It was here that they found something horrible, something never intended to be found. Something tossed away like trash and without remorse, and with the intent of no one ever seeing the beauty in this woman again.

Our story begins many days before Ike and Rusty's fishing trip, and many days before the events that led to their tragic discovery.

Monica Jeffers

*M*y office address is officially listed as 149 Union Avenue – L6, which means I occupy office 6 - located just off the lobby of The Peabody Hotel – Memphis, Tennessee. I actually would consider my address to be 3rd avenue – not Union, but the address has its perks.

The location itself is also handy. All my phone calls come through the hotel operator, which is also my answering service. I eat lunch and breakfast in the employee dining room at a great price. I have a beautiful lobby to greet potential clients - and please don't forget the duck show, it happens twice a day. Aside from the perverts who hang out in the lobby restrooms, I can't find a lot of fault with my office arrangements.

Besides, this is 1962 and people are accustomed to the modern ways of doing business. Appearance is everything, or at least a close second to whatever is first. The new real estate buzz is 'location, location, location' – I think I have one of the best.

The hotel directory and telephone yellow pages show L6 occupied by '*The Drake Detective Agency*'. That can be confusing, because the name on my office door reads:

Carson Reno – Private and Confidential Investigations

I am Carson Reno and always have been. There has never been a Drake working from this office, or any other in Memphis, that I am aware of. However, when I opened the agency I just could not find any rhyme or rhythm in 'The Reno Detective Agency'. Besides, everybody who has watched Perry Mason knows Paul Drake and who knows – people may think this is a branch office or something. A little free publicity and promotion never hurt any business, just as long as they call or show-up with money.

A large number of my clients consist of damaged spouses looking for dirt and evidence on the unfaithful partner. It is possible that infidelity has made me what I am today – not a rich man but I can pay my bills. Occasionally, I get some insurance investigation work – searching for someone who has successfully snookered the insurance company for their own goodwill, or some poor smuck who filed false claims and skipped. But mostly I deal with the underbelly of our society – where you find some very bad people and never make friends with anyone.

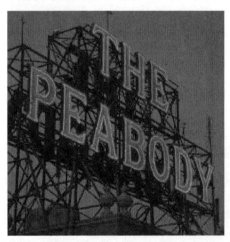

When I'm not specifically working on a case, I try to spend as much time as possible in or near the office. Another advantage of the Peabody is having access to restaurants, bars, shops and the downtown activity – so staying close is never a problem.

Afternoons and early evenings will usually find me at the *Starlight Lounge* – just off Winchester. Not only is it a good place to 'hang-out', it is a great place to look for clients or – in fact – look for those my clients have hired me to find! The *Starlight* has live entertainment starting at Noon daily – yes, I said Noon. Every day it's loaded with housewives who use the early part of the afternoon and evening to visit The *Starlight* for some drink and dance before the husband comes home from work. They cook dinner early, put it in the oven and dance on over the *Starlight* for an afternoon of wine and martinis. I have a friend who calls the place "Club Menopause" – I think that is an appropriate name.

Of course with the ladies come the men – generally just in search of some companionship, but sometimes in search for much more. Regardless, these are my clients, or potential clients, and I see no harm in getting to know as many of them as possible.

Rita is the head hostess at the *Starlight* and works some unbelievable hours. In fact, I don't remember a time when she wasn't the first to greet me – regardless of the time. She was once crowned Miss Memphis and, as I understand, had a brief acting career. This lady hasn't lost a thing with age – she still has those terrific looks and manner that won her so many awards and titles. No question, she is one knockout and classy lady who knows her stuff and knows her customers. Rita always makes sure I get an opportunity to 'meet and greet' those who are in 'distress' and might need my services. She's so good at it that I should put her on the payroll – assuming I had a payroll! However, I do make sure she gets tipped properly – whenever I get the opportunity.

My other hangout is home – or close to it. Home is a 12th floor one bedroom apartment at the 750 Adams Complex on Manassas. A great place to call home - they have a small grocery/deli on the ground floor and a little bar in the basement called the *'Down Under'*. Regardless of your condition, it is always just a short elevator ride home – and sometimes that makes good sense. Every weekend they offer live entertainment to a usually packed house. Being small, space is usually limited - but my friend 'Andy', the bartender, can always seem to find me room.

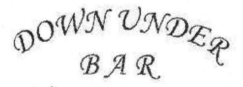

~

$\mathcal{T}$oday I was having my weekly lunch date with my lawyer and partner, Jack Logan, at the *Rendezvous*.

Over a rib sandwich and a couple of beers Jack gave me the latest update on a few shared clients. He also brought me up to speed on his involvement with Judy Strong and Maxwell Trucking in Humboldt – friends from my recent adventure titled *'Murder in Humboldt'*. Things were looking good. It seemed that Mary Ellen would be able to save the business and, along with Judy's help, put Maxwell Trucking back on the right track. Mary Ellen and Judy would jointly run the business with Judy eventually assuming full control, when all legal issues had been settled. Jack had worked hard on her case, and I certainly think his 'personal interest' in Judy had made the work much easier than normal.

While finishing lunch, Jack mentioned that he had acquired another client from the Humboldt area and would be requiring my assistance. He promised to stop by later today with the details.

I walked back across Union to my office and stopped by the front desk to pick up my mail which was unusually small - just two letters and the regular junk.

Evidently Marcie was hiding behind her large desk, because when I tossed the junk mail and started to walk away I heard her voice coming from somewhere. "Hey handsome...you've got a client waiting for you. I put her in your office, and she's not just ANY client."

"Oh yeah...who is it?" I think Marcie knows everybody, or at least thought she did. "And where are you?" I was peeking over the desk looking for her.

"It's the mayor's wife, or rather the ex-mayor's wife – since he didn't get reelected."

"That's interesting. Did you get her name? And why are you hiding?"

"I'm not hiding. I'm just...well I'm just staying out of sight until things calm down."

"What do you mean 'calm down'?" She wasn't making much sense.

Marcie ignored my question. "Your client's name is Monica Jeffers – I guess Mrs. Brian Jeffers would be a better way to put it.

She's a looker, if you know what I mean," Marcie giggled, while still hiding behind her desk..

"Yes Marcie, I do know what you mean by 'looker'." Even though I really didn't know what she meant. "Now, are you going to come out from your hiding place?"

"And she's got a dog with her."

"She's got a what?"

"A DOG...you know the little four legged furry things with tails that wag."

"Did you put the dog in my office too?"

"Well, no...not actually. I mean...I didn't, Mason did. After the dog ran all the ducks out of the fountain, then he chased them up and down the mezzanine stairs several times. Mason finally got his hands on the dog and put it in your office. What a fiasco!"

"Oh Lord!" I sighed. "Is that why you're hiding behind your desk?

"Seemed like a good idea at the time. There were ducks flying and running everywhere, the dog barking and chasing ducks, feathers flying, guests running for cover and Mason chasing that stupid dog like a chicken chasing a worm. I think it would still have been going on, except the elevator operator left his doors open, and the ducks finally ran in there for cover. They were ready to go back to the roof, and I don't blame them. You didn't notice they weren't in the fountain when you came in?"

"No damn it. I wasn't looking for the ducks. Marcie, sometimes your thought process is simply amazing. What kind of dog is it? Do you know?"

"I have no idea, just a little white dog. Cute, but loud and has no discipline," she added.

"And is it now in my office?" I frowned.

"Yes, along with Mrs. Jeffers – who I hope has better manners than her dog."

Marcie finally stood up and looked around the lobby – I assume to see if the disruption and danger had passed.

"Did you vote for the guy – her husband?" She asked, after arranging her dress and sitting down where she belonged. "Maybe she's working something political and needs to know how you voted."

"I doubt that." I shrugged. "She's probably collecting for some charity and is here to hit me up for a donation."

"Well...did you?" Marcie was shuffling through some papers on her desk.

"Did I what?"

"Did you vote for her husband?"

I thought for a moment. "I really don't recall whether I did or not, but if she asks I'll tell her yes. But I want to find out why she's really here I suppose I'll just need to talk with Monica – Mrs. Jeffers, to find out – won't I?"

"Yes, but be very careful. As I said, she's a looker and probably nothing but trouble...if you know what I mean," Marcie giggled.

"Yes Marcie. I know what you mean." This time I DID know what she meant. And as it turns out, Marcie was right – she usually is.

New Clients

*M*ason 'Booker-T' Brown is the headman around the Peabody – nobody questions that. The labor union just describes him as 'Head Porter' – but Mason takes care of everything. In addition to being totally responsible for the ducks, he makes and coordinates all work schedules for the doormen, elevator operators, porters and parking garage workers. If you aren't a maid or a cook, you best look to Mason for instructions – he is the man.

I was unhappy that Mason had put that dog in my office, but guess he didn't have much choice. I'd talk to him about that later.

~

I cautiously walked into my office and introduced myself. I immediately understood what Marcie meant by a 'looker'.

At about 5' 5" and 105 pounds, Monica Jeffers was well put together and handling her age well – which I guessed to be about 45. Other than being a little wide at the hips, Monica had taken good care of all her other parts and pieces. She had long dark hair, dark eyes and an everlasting tan, which added emphasis to a woman who had the 'air' of importance about her. This woman had 'high society' written across all her parts, looks and mannerisms. She also had a small white dog in her lap – which, I think, helped with my first impression.

She spoke first and her voice fit her description. "Mr. Reno, I am confused."

"Please, how may I 'UN-confuse' you?" I think I knew where this was going.

"Your friend Rita, at the Starlight, suggested I discuss my problems with you. But I couldn't find a Carson Reno on the hotel directory or even in the phone book – just on the door of this office. Do you work for the *Drake Detective Agency*? I certainly didn't get that impression from Rita. I feel rather odd asking, but something is strange."

"Mrs. Jeffers, please don't feel that way – it confuses everyone. Rita should have explained it to you. I own and operate the Drake Detective Agency. I AM the *Drake Detective Agency* – there is no one else. The name was just the result of my not wanting to use my name, Carson Reno, as the agency title. I realize it is odd to some, but I assure you I offer quiet and discrete investigations. I would be happy to provide some client references, if you desire."

"Rita is reference enough for me. She and I go way back, probably further than each of us want to remember. And please call me Monica – I hate that Mrs. Jeffers tag. It seems I hear it too much already."

"And please call me Carson," I said with a big smile. "Now that we have the formalities out of the way, please tell me how can I help you?"

At this point, she took the dog from her lap and put it on the floor. It immediately headed for my beautiful fake rubber plant that always sits in the corner of my office. With no outside windows, the only natural light I have is through my glass door and glass office front that face the South lobby entrance – so a plastic plant was the only option if I wanted a plant. A former client had given me the rubber plant as a 'thank-you' for a job well done, and I really enjoyed its company.

"Carson, I need to apologize for Daisy – oh, I forgot to introduce you," she interrupted herself. "This is my dog Daisy."

I wasn't sure how to introduce myself to a dog. I love dogs and love all animals, but have never been instructed on proper etiquette for an introduction to a dog.

So, I just said, "Hi, Daisy. Welcome to my office and welcome to the Peabody." But, for some reason I don't think Daisy was listening to me – she was studying my rubber plant.

"Daisy was a 'bad dog' when we came into the hotel. I'm afraid she got after the ducks and chased them all over the lobby. If it hadn't been for that nice man, 'Booker something', I'm afraid she might've hurt them."

"That would have been Mason Brown. Around the hotel he is known as 'Booker –T'. Yes, he is a very nice man and I suggest you extend your apology to him – not me. He is the one who cares for the ducks."

"I will do that, thank you for telling me," she said, dismissing my suggestion. "Now Carson, as to why I am here. I need a divorce and I need your help."

"Monica, I don't do divorces. I do discrete investigations which sometimes involve gathering information on unfaithful partners – which I provide to my clients and their attorneys. If you need one, I do know some good lawyers who specialize in that kind of thing. Would you for like me to recommend one?" She never flinched.

Glancing at Daisy while I spoke, I noticed that she had started to nibble at the lower leaves of my rubber plant. This dog had probably never seen a 'fake' plant, and didn't understand why it had no taste. So she continued to chew on one leaf, and then move to another.

"The last thing I need is another lawyer or to even KNOW another lawyer. My life has been full of lawyers for the past 20 years, and I certainly don't need another one. No...what I should have said is that I, and one of those damn lawyers I mentioned, need your special talents. I need dirt. I need names. I need photos. I need names, dates and places. I need evidence to crucify that son-of-a-bitch Brian Jeffers."

Monica Jeffers was one unhappy spouse. And, based upon what I saw sitting across from my desk, she is not someone I would want to get on my bad side.

Meanwhile Daisy continued to eat my rubber plant.

"Okay," I nodded. "That is something the *Drake Detective Agency* can handle for you. However, I'm going to need some specific information. Why don't we walk over to the restaurant and have some coffee while you tell me about it?"

"I'm afraid I shouldn't take Daisy out into the hotel just yet, she is still quite upset. Can we just have coffee here in your office?"

What about the DUCKS? Did she think they might still be quite upset too?

"Absolutely," I picked up the phone and ordered coffee delivered. Daisy had now progressed up to the second layer of leaves and seemed quite content to continue her attack on my rubber plant. If she was 'quite upset', it definitely wasn't affecting her energy and interest in my beautiful plant.

~

Over the next hour Monica shared things with me that only a woman looking for revenge would do. As a successful criminal attorney, and as Memphis Mayor for 6 years, it seemed that Brian Jeffers had sowed a lot of wild oats across Shelby County.

Monica had held her tongue and tolerated what most women would not. Since none of these oats had seemed to sprout, she expected he would eventually get tired of his ways and settle down. Half-way into his second term as mayor, Brian was doing just that. He was settling down. However, after he lost the election for a third term, something happened to change that. One of his closest aides died under strange circumstances – he fell off the roof of the 100 North Main building! The coroner had ruled accidental death. But, at least privately, Brian had never accepted that. The aide's name was Barry 'Butch' Lassiter, and a valuable resource to Brian Jeffers. Following his death his wife, Darlene, took over her husband's duties. It seems she also began to take on a more active role in the new mayor's office and a more active role with Brian, as he transitioned out of office. So active that they traveled together, took extended trips for business and seemed to always be seen together. Monica was absolutely certain that this was not just jealousy on her part – she actually believed Darlene was in complete control over Brian and the mayor's office. After her husband's death, Darlene didn't go away – she just got closer to Brian. So close that Monica had ordered Brian to move out of their home – which he had done over a week ago. Her attempts to follow him didn't work, and that's why she was sitting in my office.

"Can you help?" she asked in a very businesslike voice.

"I can certainly try. Let me do some background work and I'll get back to you in a couple of days. Will that be OK?"

"It will. What do you charge?" She asked just like she was hiring me to paint her house.

Daisy had now completely destroyed my rubber plant. There were little green plastic pieces scattered all over the floor, and obviously these were once the beautiful leaves from my plant. Should I add the cost of one fake rubber plant to my quote?

"I get $100 a day plus expenses. Is that acceptable?"

"Definitely," she answered quickly. With that, she stood up and handed me a business card with just her name and phone number.

Monica Jeffers
901-463-9893

"I'll have a contract drawn up for your signature the next time we meet," I said graciously.

She nodded acceptance and we agreed to talk in a day or two. She picked up Daisy, walked out of my office and then out of the Peabody Hotel through the 2nd Avenue exit. She never mentioned my poor rubber plant.

~

I grabbed a rolling trashcan from the lobby and deposited what was left of my beautiful plant. I also added all the small pieces Daisy had left – making sure my plant could at least get a decent burial with all it former parts. Resisting the urge to cry, I pledged to have a drink later in its honor.

Satisfied that I had done all I could for my poor rubber plant, I went back to the mail. One letter was from my fraternity, Pi Kappa Alpha, reminding me that payment was now due on my UT season ticket package. I needed to take care of that – college football was a vice I was proud to have.

The other letter was postmarked Humboldt, and return addressed to Mary Ellen Maxwell. It was an invitation to a birthday party for her son, Lewis. He was turning 21 and she was planning a large event – happening at both her residence and the Humboldt

Country Club. I wasn't sure this was something I wanted to do, but since it was RSVP, I needed to let her know my answer.

While I was pondering my decision, Jack entered the office.

"Hey buddy," he said with a questioned look on his face. "Sorry I'm late, but I got tied up on the phone. Where are the ducks? They get put up early today?"

"Yes, I suppose so." I wasn't going there with him – but am I the only one who wouldn't notice the ducks weren't in the fountain? "No problem, I've been busy myself. Now, tell me about this client you need some help with."

Jack took a seat in one of my leather office chairs. "I've been retained by a Mrs. Kathy Ledbetter. Her former employer – the Bosley Buick dealership of Milan, Tennessee has charged her with embezzlement. Are you familiar with them?"

"Yep, I have certainly heard of them, but haven't ever done any business there...that I remember. I was always a Ford man myself, stability and reliability over luxury – as my Dad always told me."

"Apparently they have been around a while and are quite respected in the area."

"Yep, and as I recall they are a large dealership serving several counties across West Tennessee."

"That's the story I got too. Mrs. Ledbetter had been bookkeeper at the business for over 12 years. One day the two owners walked into her office with the sheriff and had her arrested. I've stalled the preliminary hearing, and she's free on a $100,000 bond – but I need some ammunition for the judge to keep her out of jail."

"Interesting...what's her story?" I asked.

"Complete innocence. Her husband, Sam, is a shop foreman at the AT&T plant in Milan. They live modestly, and I've not been able to find one evil thing either of them has done."

"What about the money?" Now I was curious.

"It's missing all right. An external audit has uncovered 2 million dollars missing over the course of the last 5 years. But if Kathy and Sam have the money, they have it well hidden. Carson, I believe her. I believe she's innocent and, for some reason, is being set up."

"But...why her?"

"Good question and one somebody will answer when we get to the preliminary hearing. But, she is an obvious culprit – one of a limited few who had the opportunity and authority to skim money from the business."

"The others with the opportunity and authority would be the owners...right?"

"Right...the owners are Charles and Carlon Bosley – brothers. They've owned and operated the business for the past 25 years at the same location."

I thought for a moment before responding. "Jack...who requested the audit? Was it a routine matter of business, or something that came from a vendor or supplier request?"

"Carson, you are one sharp guy. The audit was requested by GMAC, their primary auto loan lender, and they also hold the floor plan on their cars."

"So, you smelled the same rat I did – correct?"

"Correct, and I need you to look into it and see what you can come up with. Find something I can take to the hearing and maybe get this thing dismissed before it ever gets started. I have a hunch the owners are stalling and, for some reason, are using Kathy Ledbetter as a delay to the inevitable. I hate to ask you to go back to Humboldt – but somehow I don't think you'll mind that much."

"Ha! Well it just so happens I have here on my desk a formal invitation to a party in Humboldt. Perhaps I'll just make that party and use it as an excuse to look into the Ledbetter/Bosley case. Will that be okay with you?"

"Yep...keep me up to date – you know the routine." Jack stood up, walked to the door and pointed toward the corner where my wonderful plant once home. "By the way, what happened to your plastic rubber plant?"

"It died – lack of water."

"A plastic plant? Are you crazy?"

"Yes, I am crazy. Go away. I'll call you when I make my trip."

As quickly as he closed the door, Marcie opened it.

"My, you are a busy man today. Has Mrs. 'Ex-Mayor' already left?" she asked looking around.

"Yes, and she took that mutt Daisy with her."

"So that's what she was yelling – 'Daisy'. I couldn't understand what she was yelling across the lobby while that dog was chasing the ducks. Funny."

"Not really. Marcie, please take this invitation from Mrs. Mary Ellen Maxwell and offer my positive RSVP. Do whatever it is you do – send a note, phone, letter or whatever. Just tell her I would be happy to attend. Okay?"

"Can do, and I'll also put it on your calendar." Marcie pointed to the empty corner formally occupied by my rubber plant. "By the way – what happened to your rubber plant?"

"It died – lack of water."

"Water...I thought it was a plastic plant?"

"It was. Just go away and send that RSVP. I'm headed down to the public library and then to the Starlight for the rest of the afternoon. I will see you tomorrow."

Marcie left, still staring at the empty corner my plastic rubber plant once called home.

~

I stopped at the Memphis Public Library. If I didn't find what I wanted here, I would run over and look in the *Commercial Appeal* archived files.

If you didn't know it already, reading the newspapers would tell you these are strange, tough and violent times. Our President, John Kennedy, is on the verge of sending federal troops to the University of Mississippi to protect James Meredith. Some countries, mostly our country, were conducting a nuclear test explosion in some remote part of the world every week. If that wasn't enough, President Kennedy has issued a blockade of Cuba - stopping all shipping into and out of the Cuban port of Havana. Besides making it difficult for me to get Cuban cigars, I believed this situation would have much more serious consequences.

But, I was looking for local news surrounding Barry 'Butch' Lassiter and his accidental death. There were many articles by a number of reporters, but most of those were printed immediately after the incident, and were thin and full of speculation. I located one interesting article by a Watson Clark who seemed to have some inside information, but for some reason, the details around that information never made it to print. He hinted that the political problems surrounding city and county consolidation could have been behind the incident, and would definitely have been a topic of discussions at the roof top meeting. I needed to talk with Mr. Clark.

The facts of the incident, as reported, seemed simple. It was a political fund-raiser for Brian Jeffers. At some point during the cocktail party, Barry Lassiter became drunk and accidentally fell over the railing – falling 300 feet to his death. End of story.

Reported present at the fund raiser were (among others):

Brian Jeffers - Mayor

Roger Thurbush – Vice Mayor (now the newly elected mayor)

Barry Lassiter – Chief Aide

Darlene Lassiter – Wife of Barry Lassiter

Steve Carrollton – Major contributor to Mayor Jeffers

Susan Oakley – Mayor's political advisor

Sandra Thurbush –Wife of vice mayor

Randy Price – Mayor's bodyguard

Chuck Hutchinson – Memphis Police Chief

Carlton Scruggs – Shelby County Sheriff

And if you can believe this:

Bubba Knight – Associate of Steve Carrollton

Bobby James – Associate of Steve Carrollton

Steve Carrollton was currently in jail. He had been indicted on a Federal weapons charge, stemming from incidents related to stealing weapons from military institutions. That was a part of my investigation of *'Murder in Humboldt'*.

He was also known as the head of the 'Memphis Mafia', with a center of operations on Beale Street. I was familiar with Steve and his criminal operations, and surprised to see him as a major contributor to Brian Jeffers.

Bubba and Bobby were the strong arm of Steve's operation, and we had previously had some unfriendly contact. I didn't know their current whereabouts.

I made note of the names of those at the fundraiser, with plans to talk with as many of them as I could.

~

*H*appy hour (2PM – 4 PM) had long passed by the time I reached the Starlight. Rita seated me at my usual table and promised to make sure my waitress, Ruthie, got me a Jack and Coke as quickly as possible. As she walked away, I asked her to join me when business permitted – she agreed.

I know I have said this before, but Rita is one class act. She was a former beauty queen and once crowned Miss Memphis. This lady hasn't lost a thing with age – she still has those terrific looks and manner that won her so many awards and titles. I must also add that she is one of my best friends.

Rita casually sat down, while directing one of the other hostesses to handle the door. "Well, handsome, what can we do for you? You are well behind schedule – tough day?"

"Yes, I lost a close friend today."

"Oh NO! I am so sorry. What happened?"

"They were eaten by a small white dog."

"Carson, what are you talking about?"

"Never mind…I'll share the details with you some other time. But tell me about Monica Jeffers. I saw her today and she said she had talked with you. Is she a friend?"

"In fact – yes. She and I went to Whitehaven High together and did some beauty pageants in our earlier years. I even had her daughter enrolled in my 'beauty training school' a few years ago. The daughter has moved on and gotten married, I understand, but Monica and I have remained close. She has a lot of baggage, mostly from that asshole, Brian, but I think of her as a friend and basically good people."

"Beauty School…when do you find time to do that? I never knew you not be standing at this front door!"

"Well, we all must make ends meet. It's something I've been doing for a few years, and only during the mornings and evenings I have off. I mostly work with young girls who want to join the beauty review circuit. Not a big deal, but something I enjoy."

"I never knew and, as I have always said, you amaze me." I was honest.

"Please help Monica if you can," Rita was squeezing my hand. "She's in more trouble than she probably revealed to you. It's political, and unless she gets rid of Brian, it will probably spill over to her personally."

"Other than what you have said and what she told me, is there anything that I should know before I go kicking over political cans?"

"No. But I promise to stay in touch with her and feed any information back to you. That okay?"

"Certainly, and you know it is. I'm going to start looking into the death of Barry Lassiter and see where that takes me. You think that's a good idea?" I asked seriously.

"Excellent idea," Rita said smiling. "But, now I've got to relieve Ruthie at the front door. I'll watch over you and talk with you later." She started to leave and then turned back.

"You asked me about my 'beauty training school'. Did you know I once had an ex Humboldt Strawberry Princess enrolled?"

"No, but I don't spend a lot time in Humboldt. Who was it?"

"Charlotte Luckey. She had promise, but spent too much time chasing the men – if you know what I mean?"

"I do know what you mean, but I don't remember the name. However, that's not unusual."

"Gotta' go. See you later." Rita went back to work.

~

*T*he crowd seemed dull at the '*Starlight*' and I didn't see any potential clients. After saying goodnight to Rita, I got in the Ford and made my way to the *'Down Under'* to finish the evening with Andy. They were crowded, but I hadn't eaten, and decided on one of Andy's hamburgers for my late dinner. He had his new jukebox in operation, and playing 'Little Eva' singing 'The Loco-Motion' over and over and over again.

I had a Jack and Coke with my dinner – then took the elevator home. It had been a productive day. The *Drake Detective Agency* had two new clients, and both cases should be easily handled – or so I thought!

Feeling good about today's activities, I took a shower and called it an early day. The bed felt good and I slept well – it would be the last time for a while.

Unfortunately, the next few days would turn out to be anything but easy – they would be some of the most difficult of my career.

Watson Clark

I stopped by the Commercial Appeal building on my way into the office. The receptionist informed me that Watson Clark no longer worked for the paper. Evidently, he had resigned unexpectedly a few weeks after the Barry Lassiter incident. I guess that was the reason I couldn't locate any additional details to match with his initial reporting of the death.

She had no idea where I could locate Watson, but offered to ask around among his former close friends. I left her my card and asked her, or anyone, to call me if they knew how I might locate him. She seemed nice and agreed to call if she found out anything.

~

*M*ason Brown was the first person I met as I entered the Peabody lobby.

"Mason, I understand you had some excitement around here yesterday."

"Yes sir Mr. Reno – we certainly did. That is the most excitement these ducks have had since that hen laid her eggs in one of the potted plants."

"Huh?" I frowned.

"Yep, she laid her eggs in one of the lobby planters. I tried every way I knew to get that hen outta' that planter – she wouldn't budge. That duck was not leaving those eggs."

"What did you do?"

"Well sir, I put that planter, along with the hen and her eggs on the elevator every evening and took it to the roof. Next morning, I'd put them back on the elevator and bring them back to the lobby. I did that for two weeks until she finally hatched those eggs. Mr. Reno, that was the most stubborn duck I had ever dealt with!"

"Mason, I know there is a lesson to be learned about women somewhere in that story…there must be," I laughed."

As I turned to head toward Marcie's switchboard Mason yelled, "Mr. Reno – we were cleaning your office this morning and your rubber plant is missing. What happened to it?"

"It died – lack of water." Mason just looked at me and scratched his thin gray hair.

It seems everybody was concerned about my rubber plant. Well…most everybody anyway.

When Marcie finished her call I asked, "Any messages?"

"No. Here's your mail and I want you to know that I am very very mad at you."

"Why? What did I do?"

"If you needed your plant watered, why didn't you ask? You just let it die and I would have been happy to have taken care of it for you," she was serious!

I just stood there. What could I say?

"And Carson, you will need a tux for this event in Humboldt. I'm sure yours is 'in the cleaners', so walk on over to Lee's and have him fit one for you. You've only got a couple of days."

"A tuxedo? You're kidding…right?"

"I am not kidding. So scoot yourself over there – it won't take him long."

Lee was a tailor and owned a tuxedo and bridal shop located just off the Peabody Hotel lobby. Fortunately, I'm a common size and Lee said he could have it ready for me tomorrow and would leave it in my office.

I'm not a tuxedo guy. But one thing was certain; probably no one would recognize me at the party. Guess that was good – I think.

~

*T*oday's mail was uninteresting, a few window envelopes and some advertisement flyers about the upcoming Cotton Carnival. Just as I was tossing them in the trash – the phone rang. It was Marcie.

"I have a call for you, but they won't give me a name," she blurted. *"I hate people like that."*

"Me to, but guess I better take the call. Go ahead and put it through."

I answered, "Hello, this is Carson Reno. How may I help you?"

A male voice that sounded shaky and a couple of octaves above normal spoke, *"Are you Carson Reno the private detective?"*

"Yes, and to whom am I speaking?"

"Never mind who I am. Are you the guy looking for Watson Clark?"

"I'm the Carson Reno that stopped by the Commercial Appeal office this morning and asked for Watson Clark – if that's what you mean."

"Yes...yes I guess that's what I mean. Listen, Watson and I were/are good friends. We've worked together for over 10 years and...and I'm really concerned about him." In addition to speaking a few octaves above normal, his voice was very shaky. This guy was either nervous or scared out of his wits.

"Concerned in what way?"

"Let's just say I'm concerned...very concerned. Can you...can you help him?"

"First, I would need to find him, and second, I would need to know what kind of help he needed. You're talking, but you're not saying much."

"I know, but...but I don't want to get him in trouble."

This conversation was going in circles. "Look, whoever you are. First, you want to know if I can help him and then you say you don't want to get him in trouble. Either you tell me where I can find Watson Clark or I'm hanging up. Okay?"

"I'll...I'll have to draw you a map." His voice was getting shakier.

"A map! Can't you just give me an address or phone number?" This was getting stranger by the minute.

"I don't know the address, and he ain't got a phone. You want the map or not?"

"Okay...okay a map it will be. Where can I meet you?"

"You can't. I'll have someone drop the map off at your office."

"When?"

"Within the hour," he answered quickly.

Before I could again ask him his name – he hung up.

I dialed Marcie's extension.

"Marcie, within the hour, someone will be delivering a map for me. When they get here, ring me and stall them – somehow. I need to talk with the person delivering the map. Okay?"

"A map? What kind of a map? Maybe buried treasure?" she giggled.

"I don't know. Just stall them if you can, please."

"Okay, I'll try," she snapped.

~

*F*ifteen minutes later Marcie called. *"A guy is here with an envelope and he says he needs to deliver it to you personally."*

"Super. I'll be right there."

My disappointment was quickly evident. The guy with the envelope was a messenger – one of many who move documents quickly around the downtown area – mostly by bicycle.

"Where did you pick up this envelope?" I asked the young, man who was wearing shorts and a funny hat.

"At the Commercial Appeal reception desk. They called dispatch and placed an order for a pick-up with delivery to Carson Reno at the Peabody Hotel. Are you Carson Reno?"

I responded with a 'yes' and handed him my business card along with a dollar tip. He left with a 'thank-you'. My plan for identifying the mysterious caller hadn't worked.

~

*B*ack in my office I opened the brown 8 ½ by 11 envelope. Inside was a small white envelope with my name printed on the front.

I opened the smaller envelope, but I didn't find a map. Instead I found hastily printed driving instructions. They read:

West Memphis to Interstate 55 North. Take the Turrell exit and drive West on Hwy. 63 through Marked Tree. Then take Hwy. 14 West toward Harrisburg. Drive 4 miles and turn left – south on State Rd 373. Drive one mile then turn left – east on Buckhorn, a dirt road. Drive ½ mile and then turn right – south on Collier Lane, a dirt road. Follow Collier Lane until it dead ends. There you will find a dirt driveway and a mailbox that reads Amos Duncan. Follow the driveway until you come to a yellow house trailer.

That was it? No indication of what or who I would find at the Amos Duncan residence? I'm thinking, "This is crazy."

But, I guess I'm just crazy enough to follow these idiot directions – or certainly curious enough anyway. Besides, it was a nice day for a drive in the Arkansas countryside.

~

I still drive a 56 Ford – left over from college. It's black, 4 doors, V8, manual transmission and nothing fancy. It is however, very functional and very dependable – not to mention it's built like a tank. It is also very fast – fast enough to get you into trouble quick, and hopefully, fast enough to get you out of trouble just as quickly.

I put my old Ford on the road, driving across the Mississippi River Bridge, through West Memphis and then north on Interstate 55. It really was a nice day for a drive, and once you leave the populated area of West Memphis, there wasn't much to look at but flatland, rice fields and wild ducks.

As I'm driving, I'm wondering what would make a man leave a home and job to live in a trailer located down some dirt road in rural Arkansas? Obviously, he was hiding from something or someone, and it had to be serious enough to prompt such a radical transition. Guess I would just have to wait and ask whomever I found at the Amos Duncan residence.

~

*T*he directions were accurate. As I turned off the pavement at Buckhorn, I was amazed at just how rural this location was. No houses visible from the road, only a few scattered mailboxes and no driveways – just rice and soybean fields for as far as you could see.

At the end of Collier Lane, I found the mailbox – although I'm not sure it had seen mail in quite some time. It was barely standing and leaning seriously to the left.

I followed the driveway for only a few hundred yards before coming upon a small group of trees and a yellow house trailer parked underneath. There were no visible vehicles, so I was wondering if maybe I was on a wild goose chase – or in this case – a wild duck chase.

Amos Duncan Trailer

I parked in the shade, opened the car door and stepped out onto the grass. That's when I heard deep voice coming from somewhere behind me. "Put your hands where I can see them and don't turn around."

Of course, I immediately turned around! Bad idea.

I was facing a small man wearing faded overalls, a red plaid shirt and with a beard that covered most of his face. He was carry a double barreled shotgun, which he immediately stuck into my stomach and said quietly, "Mister, either you don't hear well or are just looking to get your insides spread all over this thing you call a car."

"Listen, my name is Carson Reno – I am a private investigator from Memphis. I need to talk with Watson Clark regarding a case I'm working on. Someone who works at the Commercial Appeal gave me directions to this place. For reasons I don't understand, that person would not identify themselves. Look, there's no way I could have found this place without directions – but apparently there has been a mistake. So, if you will remove that shotgun from my belly, I'll just get into my car and forget we ever had this conversation. Okay?"

He backed off. "I guess that would have been my friend Bernie...Bernie Taylor. Bernie and I worked together at the paper. He would have been the one who gave you directions. No one else could have."

"Are you Watson Clark?" I already knew the answer.

"Yes I am. Now...you want to tell me why you're here?"

"Is there some place we can talk – without the shotgun?" I was hoping.

He thought for a moment before answering. "Okay, let's go inside. It ain't much, but at least I can sit down while you tell me your story."

Considering the outside appearance, the inside of his trailer was not what I expected. It was well furnished and well kept. I got the feeling of a woman's presence – not sure how I could tell, but it was just too well kept for a man living alone.

I began by telling Watson my story and the reasons I wanted to talk with him. He sat calmly and listened while chain smoking Camels - showing no emotion or asking any questions.

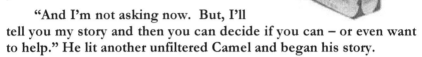

"So Watson, I am here to gather information – not here specifically to help you. You haven't asked for help, your friend Bernie did."

"And I'm not asking now. But, I'll tell you my story and then you can decide if you can – or even want to help." He lit another unfiltered Camel and began his story.

This property and trailer belonged to his wife's family – Amos and Mary Duncan of Newport, Arkansas. He and his wife, Amy, spent as much time as possible at her parents' home in Newport. But they had limited house space, so the majority of the time they stayed here at the trailer. His wife was currently in Newport, and expected to return later that afternoon.

Prior to the death of Barry Lassiter, Watson had been working an assignment story on the city/county consolidation. His digging into the story lines had not taken him straight to Brian Jeffers' mayor's office – as he had expected. Where it did take him was to Steve Carrollton's office on Beale Street. It seemed a lot of money was changing hands in order to have this consolidation go the way Steve Carrollton wanted – which was no consolidation at all. The politicians he owned – those he had bought with Memphis Mafia money, supported his interests. Brian Jeffers was evidently one of these.

Barry Lassiter had supplied much of this information to Watson. Barry and Brian Jeffers were at odds about most everything and Barry saw him as a way to get Brian out of office and, hopefully, in jail. Watson and Barry had put together a significant file on corruption surrounding the mayor's office and had plans to deliver the file to the DA. The day before that delivery, Barry took his fall from the 100 North Main building. Watson had also been at that cocktail party, but didn't witness the fall. He did, however, know that Barry was not drunk and this fall was no accident. The facts stated that no one had witnessed the fall, but just before going over the rail, he had been in heated discussions with both Brian and Steve Carrollton on the balcony. He last saw Barry Lassiter with two of Steve Carrollton's associates – whose names he did not know at that time.

Watson said he had made a preliminary report on the incident, but omitted many of the details. His concern was the investigation or lack of investigation by Chuck Hutchinson's police department. Then his concerns and fears got worse. He admitted he was just too afraid to take his file to the DA – and decided to wait until things cooled. They didn't.

Bubba Knight and Bobby James showed up at his house one night after midnight. They beat him up, knocked around his wife and ransacked their house. They were looking for the file, and they found it. Bubba and Bobby also left him with the message that if another copy of this file existed – it would be used in his obituary. Watson and Amy had gotten the message. They packed up and slipped out of town in the middle of the night.

I had questions.

"Does another copy of this file really exist?"

"Yes, but I wish it didn't." I don't think he wanted to tell me that.

"Okay, we'll come back to that later. Where does Darlene Lassiter fit into this story?"

"I'm not sure. But I do know she shed very few tears at the funeral. I figure she had plans to follow the money and stay as close to Brian as possible – I understand she has done just that. Am I right?"

"Possibly," I thought for a moment before asking the real question. "Watson, how do I get my hands on that file?"

"You don't, and if I ever get my hands on it again, it won't exist! We have made ourselves comfortable here – or at least as comfortable as we can be. I don't intend for my wife or myself to have an unfortunate accident – do you understand?"

"I do understand. But if I can find you a way out of this and a way to get your lives back to normal – without fear from any of the Mafia hoods – would you turn the file over to me and the DA?"

"I'll think about it. Now, I need you to leave. My wife will be home soon and I don't want her to know you were here. She believes no one can find us here, and I would just as soon keep her believing that."

"Okay," I said headed to the front door. "Here's my card and phone number. Please call me if anything else comes to mind or if anyone tries to contact you. Meanwhile, I have some ideas that just might lead to a solution, and find a way to get you and Amy back where you belong."

Drake Detective Agency
Peabody Hotel - Memphis, TN

Carson Reno
Private Investigator
MA(dison) 3 - 6878

"Right now we belong here," he said frankly. "Please leave and lose those driving directions – understand?"

"I understand," I said over my shoulder and getting back in the Ford.

I rolled down my windows and put the nose of the Ford into the wind. It was a nice fall day, and I would enjoy a slow drive back to Memphis.

I had already reached Interstate 55 by the time Amy arrived back at the Amos Duncan trailer. She had brought a pot roast from her mothers and a fresh carton of Camels for Watson – he was a chain smoker.

*T*he bomb had been placed behind the trailer and strategically close to the propane tanks that furnished cooking fuel and heat. What the bomb didn't destroy, the fire did. When someone finally discovered the tragedy, nothing remained but scorched ground and smoldering metal where the Amos Duncan trailer had once been. The fire had gotten hot enough to burn Amy's car and most of the trees in the area. With no neighbors, it would be two days before anyone missed Amy and Watson – and only then because Amy had not called her parents as promised.

~

*M*y drive back to Memphis went quickly and without incident. My first thought was to call Monica and tell her what I had discovered, but it was too early in the investigation for that. I think I'll concentrate on Mr. Brian Jeffers and see what he has been up to since leaving office. I knew Steve Carrollton was in jail, but things like that usually had little effect on underworld activity. Either they ran it from jail or someone else quickly took their place. I also had the feeling that little had changed with the changing of the name on the mayor's office door.

The Manhattan Club

*M*arcie had already left when I finally got back to my office. She had a note posted on my office door where I COULD NOT miss it.

Call Elizabeth Teague at 901-478-2233.

It was a Memphis number, so I knew that Elizabeth Teague must be back in town. She had an apartment in Germantown, and despite placing many calls to her; we had not spoken in several weeks.

Elizabeth Teague is the kind of woman every man needed to know - at least once in his life. Taller than most, she had those kind of legs that just keep going and going. Unlike most women I meet, she had class – sometimes to her detriment, but she had class. Slim, blonde, well put together and a personality that gave your hormones a wake-up call…if not an electric shock. Liz worked for Southern Airways and was, literally, a jet setter – traveling across and around the world with her work.

I met Elizabeth Teague while working on a *'Murder in Humboldt'*. She and Mary Ellen Maxwell (the lady who had invited me to the party) were the closest of friends. Both ladies lived and operated at a level much above Carson Reno – but I felt honored to call both of them friends.

Liz and I had not really spoken since my last visit to Humboldt, and I assumed her calling was related to the upcoming party. I gave her a call.

She answered on the second ring. *"Hello, this is Liz."*

"Hello, this is Carson. Do I have a real person, or is this a recording?"

"Sweetheart, you have the real thing. Great to hear from you; thanks for calling me back."

"What can I do for you? You have a boyfriend that needs some 'go-away' muscle work, or are you calling to get an update on how the lower class lives?"

"Neither, smart-ass...I just wanted to know if you are going to make Mary Ellen's party," she snapped.

"Yep, I have plans to be in Humboldt tomorrow evening, and available for the gala event the next day. You are also going – I assume?"

"Absolutely, I wouldn't miss it. Do I need to remind you that a tuxedo is required? I'm sure yours is in the cleaners, so you might want to dust it off. Okay?"

"Done that – I am one prepared detective." I'm sure she didn't really believe that, but it felt good to say it.

"Great. I'm looking forward to seeing you again. Are you available for a drink and catch-up conversation tonight?" she asked boldly.

"Yes mam, I am available!" I definitely answered too quickly, and with way too much enthusiasm.

"Listen, handsome. Don't get your libido worked up. I've got an early flight out tomorrow and then back late so I can make it to the party. There won't be any breakfast date, so you can calm the prostate and keep your charm to yourself...this time. We have a deal?"

"Are you always this proud of yourself, or do I bring the best out of you?"

"I'm always this proud. Now, do you want to have a drink or not?"

"I do, but I'll do you one better. I need to go to the Manhattan Club this evening. Are you up to that?"

"Wow – maybe I have misjudged you, Carson Reno. I would be happy to be your guest at the Manhattan Club. I have just the outfit."

I was sure she did – and I wanted to see it!

"I'll pick you up at eight. That work?" I asked.

"Are you still driving that black thing you call a car? If so, NO you may not pick me up. I'll pick you up. Where do you live?"

I gave her my address and directions. Hey, I'm not crazy!

~

The Manhattan Club

*T*he Manhattan Club is located at 1459 Elvis Presley Blvd., and is actually just down the road from Graceland. The King has been known to rent the whole club on special occasions and throw his own 'private' parties. For us 'normal folks', it's actually an upscale supper club, which offers a full menu and name entertainment on most nights.

My hopes were to get a sighting of Brian Jeffers, and make some decisions for myself on what he might or might not be up to.

~

*A*t 8:03 that familiar red Corvette rolled into the parking area in front of my apartment building. It had barely stopped when Liz jumped out and threw those long arms around me. Her kiss was long, sincere and wet. She finished with a familiar nibble on my ear.

"Hey Carson Reno, you're as good looking as I remember," she laughed.

"And you're not bad yourself, Miss Teague." Her blonde hair was shorter than I remembered, and she was still sporting a great tan – one of those tans you can actually smell, when you get close enough. Her dinner dress was short and red - very red. Much brighter than the Corvette - if that was possible. The dress had thin narrow straps, showing just enough to tease but keep the looker wondering. With her matching high heels, I felt overpowered – I think Liz liked it like that!

I headed around to the passenger door but she beat me there.

"No sir – Mr. Reno. I don't drive on dates." With that, she tossed me the keys.

We spent the short drive catching up on recent activities and talking about Mary Ellen's upcoming party. It was hard work just talking and keeping this 327 cubic inch/four speed monster under control, while letting my eyes soak up as much of Liz as I could. She was nice to look at.

~

*T*he doorman took charge of the Corvette and our hostess took us to a table close to the dance floor, but not too close to the band. It was perfect.

50

Memphis Slim

Early evening was spent with wine, appetizers and salad. Memphis Slim was the entertainment - along with some other recording groups out of Sunny Side Records. I didn't see who I was looking for, and it seemed my search for Brian Jeffers was going to come up a zero. It was a long shot anyway – although I knew his crowd was a frequent visitor to the Manhattan Club.

Turns out I was right, but just looking in the wrong place.

We ordered steaks and Liz took the obliged trip to powder her nose. I used this opportunity to visit the bar and ask the bartender a few questions. After some simple talk I asked, "I understand a lot of famous people come in here."

"Yep, sure do – but not tonight. You're out of luck. Best we can offer tonight is an ex-mayor and some 'would-be' thugs."

"Oh, yeah," I tried to hide my enthusiasm. "You mean Ex-mayor Jeffers – right? I've looked around but haven't seen him," I offered casually.

"That's because he's not in the main dining room," the bartender replied while washing some glassed. "They're having dinner in the back – the 'Blue Room'. It's private for those who don't want to mingle with the regular folks. You need a drink?"

"Yes, a Jack and Coke please. How do you get into this 'Blue Room'?" I answered.

"You don't. Let me get you that drink," he said walking away.

Liz had returned from the powder room, and was in her seat when I got back to the table.

"Drinking again?" she frowned. "Wine not good enough for you?"

"Hey – I told you I'm working. I needed to pump the bartender, and getting a drink was part of the program. I'll save it until after dinner."

We were still waiting on our steaks, so I excused myself and pretended to search for the men's room. However, I was really looking for this 'Blue Room' -- it wasn't hard to find. In the back of the band area was a small dark hallway that led to a single door. The sign on the door read:

The Blue Room

Acting ignorant - I quickly opened the door and walked in, much like I expected to find the men's room behind the door. What I found was a room full of interesting people having a private dinner. Randy Price, the bodyguard, immediately greeted me at the door and told me this was a private party. I apologized, turned and left – but not before taking a mental note of who sat around the large dinner table located in the center of the room.

Seated at the table were:

Brian Jeffers – ex-Mayor

Darlene Lassiter – Barry Lassiter's widow

Chuck Hutchinson – Chief of Police

Carlton Scruggs – Shelby County Sheriff

Terry Davis – President of the Dock Workers Union

And two others I couldn't identify. They had their backs to me, and didn't turn around at my intrusion.

Back at the table Liz and I had our steaks, and then settled for an after dinner cocktail rather than desert.

Memphis Slim was just getting into his rhythm when the hostess seated Brian Jeffers and Darlene Lassiter at a table close to the band. I guess the dinner meeting was over.

They only sat long enough to order a drink, and then immediately hit the dance floor. He wasn't a half-bad dancer and Darlene was hanging onto him like a wet suit. She was leaving very little room between her and him – making a statement about their relationship.

I assume other members of the dinner party must have used some unseen door for their exit – because no one else made an appearance in the main dining room.

Liz and I danced to a few tunes, but we mostly just talked and got to know each other better. At midnight, she let me know it was time to go and I obliged – Brian and Darlene just seemed to be getting started.

She left me in front of my apartment building with another wet kiss, and I told her I would see her at Mary Ellen's party – if not before.

~

*A*ndy was still cleaning his bar counter when I stopped at the *'Down Under'* for a nightcap. The place was empty except for a young couple huddled up in a corner booth. The loud jukebox was playing Booker T and the MG's 'Green Onions' and Andy was timing his cleaning to the beat of the music.

"Andy, can I still get a Jack/Coke? You can put it in a travel cup – I need to use your pay phone before calling it a day."

"Who in their right mind would want to talk to you at this hour

 of the night?" he laughed.

"Probably nobody – but I know I can leave them a message."

Fortunately, the phone was located in an area where I could hear and speak over the loud music. I placed a call to Larry Parker,

Chief of Detectives for Shelby County. I knew he wouldn't be there, but central dispatch would take the message, and he should get it in the morning. The message was for Larry to call me at my office first opportunity tomorrow.

Larry had been a policeman for as long as I could remember. He worked his way up the ladder and, unlike many others, had done it through honesty and good police work. I trusted him and he had never let me down. Our friendship goes way back to the beginning. He was a sponsor for my private detective license and had always been there when I needed him – and I think I needed him again.

~

*A*ndy made me a Jack/Coke to go, and I took the elevator home. Watching the lights of Memphis from my patio, I reviewed my day before showering and going to bed – it had been interesting. Tomorrow I would travel to Humboldt and work on Jack's case, while having fun at Mary Ellen Maxwell's party. Tbings should be uneventful, and maybe Liz and I would find some time to 'strengthen' our relationship. Little did I know what events these next fews days would offer. If I did, I might have just stayed in that warm bed!

Jackson, Tennessee

3592 SUMMER AVE.
Sandy's
THRIFT AND SWIFT
DRIVE-IN
Hamburger
French Fries
Milk Shake
45¢
ALSO 779 S. HIGHLAND

*L*arry Parker had called twice by the time I walked in the north lobby door of the Peabody – it was almost eleven o'clock.

Marcie yelled across her desk, "Hey Carson, the police are looking for you this morning. A Captain Parker has already called twice. You in trouble?"

"I'm always in trouble," I shouted back, "just sometimes more in trouble than others. Did he leave a number?"

"Yes, it's on your desk, and your tux is hanging on your door."

Dispatch quickly passed me through to Larry. I told him I was headed out of town and asked if he could arrange to meet me for lunch. I promised no more than a half-hour. He agreed, and I suggested we meet at Sandy's on Summer Avenue – it was close to his office and convenient to my drive out of town.

Sandy's was new to Memphis and had grown very popular over the past few months. Hamburgers were their specialty, but they actually had a good menu, if you could get past the burgers!

As I expected Sandy's was crowded – it was lunchtime. Also, as I expected, Larry was already there when I arrived. He had claimed a window booth and was working on a Sandy's Burger and fries when I sat down.

Sandy's *Thrifty, Swift* DRIVE-IN

NOW OPEN

MENU

Delicious Beefy **HAMBURGER** 15c

CHEESEBURGERS .... Only 19c

Crisp, Golden Brown **FRENCH FRIES** 10c

Thick, Creamy **MILK SHAKES** 20c

TOASTED CHEESE 15c

SOFT DRINKS 10c

775 So. Highland
block north of Park

"You couldn't wait? I'm buying lunch – or didn't I mention that?" I hadn't.

"No you didn't. But, now that I know, I'll add a shake and some cheesecake. Thanks Buddy!"

"Not being personal Larry, but if I were you, I'd skip that shake and cake. I saw you on TV last week and there wasn't enough room for you and the reporter on the same screen. What would you dress-out now – about 250?"

"220 and you know the camera always makes you look heavier than you are. Now, I know we didn't come here to discuss my diet so let's hear it," he said before downing what was left of his burger.

"Can you think of any reasons why an ex-mayor, the Chief of Police, the Shelby County Sheriff and various other shifty characters would be having a meeting in a back room of the Manhattan Club?"

"Dinner, maybe?"

"I'm sure they had dinner, but I believe there's more to it."

"Jeez Carson, can't people have dinner in private without some mystery being involved?"

"I'm sure they can, but I need to tell you some other things."

I told Larry my story, starting with my visit from Monica, the mysterious map that evidently came from Bernie Taylor and then my crazy trip to Arkansas to see Watson Clark. I finished with my observations from last night at the Manhattan Club.

"Interesting," he said.

"Yes it is interesting. And if I can get my hands on that file, I believe we're going to see some big names take a big fall. We both know that our Memphis Mafia friends on Beale Street want no part of this city/county consolidation. The prostitution, gambling, illegal weapons, booze and drug operations would take a real hit – maybe even shut them down."

"Interesting," he said again.

"We both know a lot of money is changing hands – it has to be. Otherwise they couldn't get away with all the things they do. We just don't know 'whose' hands, and I think this file might just tell us that."

"Interesting," he said again.

"Is that all you can say – interesting!"

"Okay, Carson, what do you want me to do?"

"I want you to check out this guy Bernie Taylor – he works at the Commercial Appeal and I think he knows where this file might be. I also think he might be in danger. Watson has himself hidden away in Arkansas, and you can check on him later – he's so scared we would never get the file from him anyway. I also need you to re-open the investigation into Barry Lassiter's death. I'll offer even money that somebody threw him over that rail, and I have a pretty good guess who did it."

"You want me to make some waves – huh?"

"Absolutely not. Think up some excuse to re-open the death investigation, and keep everything on a low key – especially concerning Bernie Taylor."

"Okay – what else?" Larry asked.

"Just stay in touch. I'll be in Humboldt for a few days – you know how to reach me there. I'll be at Chief's."

"Okay...I'll call if I find anything you need to know. Otherwise, let me hear from you when you get back in town. Now, here's the check. Thanks for lunch," he said getting up to leave.

He was finished, and I still hadn't even ordered!

"Larry, there is one other thing. That fellow named Dollar you sent to the pen for running an auto theft ring – didn't he make parole and relocate to Jackson, Tennessee?"

"Alfred E. Dollar...can't ever forget that name. He had a big operation – stealing cars, changing VIN numbers, selling used cars for new, turning back mileage – this guy was a real piece of work. Yes, he made parole and relocated to Jackson, but I've not heard anything from or about him. Why?"

"Just curious. I'm working on a case for one of Jack's clients in Milan, Tennessee -- embezzlement at a car dealership, but it's got a bad smell to it. If our friend Alfred E. Dollar is in the area, he might have some information to share."

"Carson, I suggest you be careful with this guy. His name doesn't fit his personality. He's not a nice person, and I would be very surprised if he voluntary shared any information with you. And you can also bet that whoever he is currently running with isn't of much better character. Just be cautious."

"Will do. I'll stay in touch," I offered as Larry walked away.

I ordered a Sandy's hamburger to go and pointed the Ford east on Hwy. 70/79. At Brownsville I stayed on Hwy. 70 and drove toward Jackson, rather than Humboldt.

~

*B*emis is a section of Jackson's south side. If you were looking for trouble, Bemis would a good place to look. I headed for Bemis.

I figured if I had any chance of finding Alfred E. Dollar, Bemis was the best place to start. Bars and used car lots lined both sides of Hwy. 45 South, and after buying a few beers at *'Murphy's'* – I found out what I wanted to know – Alfred E. Dollar was in the area and was a regular. According to the bartender, my best bet for finding Alfred this time of day would be the Bemis Pool Room. That was my next stop.

My problem was that I didn't know what Alfred E. Dollar looked like – so I really wouldn't know if I saw him. This made my questions more difficult and very dangerous, as I was about to find out.

I sat on a stool at the bar in the poolroom for 30 minutes, and never got the feeling that Alfred E. Dollar was in the room – that was based upon the conversations going on around the bar, pool tables and domino games. Expecting the worst, I asked the biggest and ugliest fellow in the poolroom if he knew where I could find Alfred E. Dollar.

He walked over and blew his beer breath in my face as he asked, "Just who wants to know?"

"Me. I want to know. I'm the one who asked. What are you confused about?" He visibly did not appreciate my words or tone.

"Mister, are you drunk or just as stupid as you look," he leaned over and put his face only inches from mine. "Would you like for me to break your nose before or after I throw you out?"

"Those are a lot of questions – just let me answer them this way," I said backing away from his stinking breath. "I don't know Alfred E. Dollar by sight. But, what I do know is that I have two loaded car haulers parked between here and Bolivar, and I need a buyer. I was given the name Alfred E. Dollar and also given the understanding that he might have an interest. That's why I'm asking where I could find Alfred E. Dollar. Does that answer any of your questions?"

"Who's 'giving' all this information? Are you a cop?" His face was once again getting closer to mine – I'm sitting and he's standing.

"How come you keep answering my questions with more questions? Let's start over. Do you know where I can find Alfred E. Dollar?"

"No."

"Thank you for the conversation – it has been interesting. Do you have any suggestions on where I might look? Now, just so we are clear – that is a different question from my original one. Can we skip the foreplay and try for a yes or no?"

"No."

"Thank you," I said turning around on my barstool and trying to get him out of my face.

Then he added, "But if you'll leave your name and number where you can be reached, I'll see that Al gets it."

'Al'? No wonder I wasn't getting anywhere, I was using the wrong name! Anyone with a handle like Alfred E. Dollar would certainly feel better with just a simple – 'Al'. How could I have been so stupid!

"Tell you what. You tell 'Al' that my name is Carson, and I'll be staying at Chief's Motel in Humboldt for the next couple of days. If he's interested, have him call me there."

"Humboldt? I thought you said your trailers were in Bolivar? And what's your last name? He'll need that, too."

"Here we go with your questions again. No, I said they were BETWEEN here and Bolivar – not IN Bolivar. So, just let me worry about the trailer and cars. Okay? And he doesn't need to know any more than Carson – they'll know me when he calls."

"Okay. I'll give him the message." Finally he got his beer breath out of my face.

"Thanks, it has been a pleasure having this conversation. We must do it again sometime soon," I said getting off the barstool and heading toward the door.

I left while I still had all my parts. My welcome had been all used up!

~

It was already dark when I made my exit from the Bemis Pool Room; I headed straight to Chief's Motel and Restaurant to see if I could get a room. Chief's is a popular local hangout located on North 22nd. in Humboldt. It's owned and operated by a couple of close friends, Ronnie and Nickie Woodson. Given the opportunity, you would find it an unusual and terrific place to stay and visit. They offer an indoor restaurant, outside curb service and small cottage rooms for traveling guests. You can't miss it – it's located right under the big neon Indian Chief sign!

Nickie and husband Ronnie have owned and operated Chief's for as long as I can remember. He runs the kitchen and does most of the cooking. Nickie handles everything else – including Cottage rentals, the books, and the inventory and keeping Ronnie in line. Ronnie has a 'wandering eye' and probably other 'wandering' parts too – which does keep Nickie busy. However, along with a couple of waitresses, and Nickie's supervision, everything always seems to go like clockwork. She also manages the carhops who serve outside patrons.

Chief's Cottages

Carhops are a different breed – they are either good or just plain terrible. Tommy was my favorite and had been with Nickie and Ronnie since the beginning. I guess you would call him the 'team leader' carhop. Whatever you needed – and I mean 'whatever you needed' Tommy Trubush was your man. Everybody knew there was a lot of underage drinking – but Tommy kept it straight and never let it get out of hand. I have many times seen him put tough guys on the ground, and when he asked someone to leave – they left. He ran the outside show – no question about it.

This was a Friday night and Chief's was busy, as usual. I managed to slip in the door and grab a barstool before Nickie noticed. Never looking up, she walked over and asked, "What can I get for you?"

"A vodka martini – shaken, not stirred." That made her look up!

"Carson Reno, it's great to see you…I think. And who do you think you are - James Bond? We don't do martinis here, and you know it. It'll be Jack Daniel's and Coke for you, I know you. Remember?"

"Yes I do. Good to see you too Nickie. Can I get a room?"

"Sure thing, but what brings you to town? Oh, wait … I know. It's that big shindig going on tomorrow night - right?"

"How'd you guess?" I laughed.

"I run a bar – nothing gets by me. And by the way, this town hasn't been the same since the last time you were here. Please tell me you are just here for the party and not to turn this town upside down? Please?" Nickie was smiling, but serious.

"Just for the party, maybe I'll call it vacation. Would that make you happy?"

"I doubt it. Your vacations are probably just full of loose women. And come to think of it – your whole life is full of loose women."

"Be nice Nickie. How is Ronnie?" I was looking around.

"If I don't kill him tonight, he'll live to be a day older. But, the night is still young – and a lot younger than he thinks he is!"

"Understand situation normal - right?"

"Right. I'm going to put you in Cottage 4. It seems to be your favorite, and I just had a honeymoon couple check out of it this morning. You can probably still smell their 'bliss' all over the walls," Nickie was making sniffing jesters with her nose.

"Honeymoon! What kind of couple in their right mind would spend their honeymoon at Chief's? Wait – let me ask that question a different way. Did they arrive here on a tractor? If that's the case, then I'll understand."

"Mr. Reno, if you want a room tonight, you might want to change your attitude. I realize that we might not match the luxury you find in your 'Peabody Hotel', but we do offer some things our customers appreciate. Besides, who are you kidding? You've 'honeymooned' in our cabins on more than one occasion. Fact?"

"That is a fact Mrs. Woodson. Now, can I get that Jack/Coke?"

"You canceling the martini order?"

"Yes, but only because you don't have any olives," I snapped.

"Can I surprise you?" she grinned.

"No, just the Jack/Coke please."

I needed to make a call and would, of course, need to use the phone located outside. Whatever idiot installed this payphone next to the jukebox had to have been drunk or crazy – probably both. Nobody used that phone because nobody could HEAR while using that phone. The jukebox only stopped playing when Nickie or Ronnie turned it off – which was never. It probably has a thousand country songs already lined up for play. People just keep putting money in it and wondering why their song isn't playing next – it would take a week to cycle through and reach their selection. No matter, they still keep dropping quarters and punching buttons.

I yelled across the bar. "Nickie, why don't you do something about that damn jukebox?"

"Why, what's wrong with it?" she yelled back.

"What's wrong? It plays all the time – it never stops. Grinding country songs out around the clock unless you or Ronnie turn it off. Doesn't that bother you?"

"Nope, I like the music. You don't?"

"Forget it. Get me the Jack/Coke. I'll be using the outside phone," I said as I headed out the front door.

I caught Jack Logan still in his office, and shared the information about my search for Alfred E. Dollar.

"You idiot," he shouted. "You're going to get yourself hurt. These guys don't play nice – and you know that."

"Yes, I know that. But, I have an idea he's either involved or knows something about the Bosley Buick operation. Have you checked for any offshore connections to Charles and Carlon Bosley?"

"What? You thinking 'take the money and run'?"

"Well, with 2 million, you can live pretty good on some Caribbean island."

"Okay, Carson, let me look into it. Anything else?"

"Yes, I would like to visit with Kathy and/or Sam Ledbetter tomorrow. Can you set that up?"

"Can do. I'll call her tomorrow and tell her you'll be calling. You need a phone number?"

"Yes, please."

"686-5666, that's a Milan number," Jack answered quickly. "Stay in touch, and let me know how your visit goes. I've only got a couple of weeks before the preliminary hearing – so I need things to happen quickly, if they're going to happen."

I said good-by to Jack and went in search of my Jack Daniel's and Coke. As expected, Nickie had it exactly where it should be.

"Hey Nickie," I yelled over the music. "What do you know about this party tomorrow night?"

"It is a big deal. And I mean a BIG DEAL. My cousin, Ted Blaylock, runs our little airport, and they've hired him to keep it open - starting tomorrow all the way through Sunday afternoon. That's unheard of around here."

"Really," I said sipping my first Jack/Coke of the day.

"Yes. And I also understand they've hired Charlie Rich to perform at the Country Club - and only the Lord knows what else is being planned. This thing must be costing a fortune – good for our little community economy. Make those 'tight asses' turn loose of some money – spend it here instead of Miami, New Orleans or somewhere else."

"You seeing any benefits?"

"Probably will. We're booked solid and most of the names on the reservations I've never heard of. They're coming from somewhere else – not from around here."

"I know you and Ronnie are going. Who's handling Chief's while you're at the party?"

"Mr. Reno. We are edging closer to another *'Murder in Humboldt'* – and that would be your murder! Now you know damn well that Ronnie and I will NOT be attending this affair. First, we weren't invited. Second, while I could probably find something appropriate to wear, Ronnie would sure look stupid wearing his apron and jeans. He could only wear – apron and jeans – because he has nothing else to wear. That, and his birthday suit, is all I have seen him wear in the past 10 years. So, if you want to keep your room and good grace while at Chief's, I suggest you bring yourself back down to our level – where you belong. Understood?"

"Yes, 'Mam'," I was getting on Nickie's bad side – a place I did not want to be.

Sipping on my first drink, I glanced at the door when this 'oddly' dressed guy walked in Chief's. He was a big man, and his dress just didn't fit his actions or manner, jeans and a plaid shirt weren't his style - this was a tailored suit and silk tie guy. It seemed, for some reason, he was 'dressing down' to perhaps blend in or avoid attention. In my eyes, it did just the opposite.

He rented a room from Nickie, and quickly exited back through the front door.

"Who was that?" I asked Nickie when she walked over.

"Register card says Brad Knuchols – Memphis, Tennessee. You know him?"

"Looks familiar – but I'm not sure why. Is he here for the party?"

"I can't say, but suspect he is. Made a reservation last week, two men - one room. He's in Cottage 5 – next to you."

"Do me a favor. Let me know who else checks in – strangers I mean. Can you do that?"

"Probably go to jail for it, but I know a detective who can get me out…I think. Sure, I can do that. You expecting trouble?"

"No…no, not at all. But this guy doesn't fit – somehow. Wonder who made up the guest list – any ideas?"

"None. But I suspect that many of the town elite had a hand in who is and who isn't invited. I understand some of the former Strawberry Queens and Hostess Princesses will be there with family and friends. Maybe Mary Ellen is trying to get her son hitched. Nothing surprises me anymore."

I added one of Ronnie's burgers to my next drink order and reminded myself that I really needed to eat better. Burgers for every meal were not healthy.

Calling it a long day, I headed for my Cottage. The car parked in front of Cottage 5 was a dark blue 1961 Chrysler with Memphis plates. I wrote down the number, '1-4J745', with plans to have Leroy Epsee (Gibson County Sheriff) check on it later.

I unlocked my Cottage door and looked back at the cars that continued to endlessly circle Chief's. This nightly tradition would continue until the early hours of tomorrow morning. But something unusual was in this traffic jam – it was a black Cadillac limo. Chief's didn't see many limousines – tractors yes – limousines no.

It slowed in front of Cottage 5, and our Mr. Brad Knuchols exited his room and took a place in the back seat of the Caddy.

I watched as it continued to circle Chief's and eventually exited onto 22nd Avenue headed north. This was interesting, but considering tomorrow's event, I wasn't surprised. Probably some advance security for the governor or other official. I went to bed.

1961 Chrysler

1-4J745

Kathy and Sam

I grabbed a quick breakfast, a coffee to go, a handful of dimes and settled in at the pay phone out front.

My first call was to the Gibson County Sheriff, Leroy Epsee. He, of course, wasn't in. I did speak with Deputy Jeff Cole and asked him to tell Leroy I was in town and would like to buy him lunch, if possible. He agreed to give him the message, and suggested I call back sometime around noon.

My next call was to the number Jack had given me for Kathy and Sam Ledbetter – Kathy answered on the first ring. Jack had already called, told her I was in town and would want to talk with her as soon as possible. We agreed to meet this morning, and I should come right over.

I then called Captain Larry Parker to get an update and see if he'd been able to reach Bernie Taylor at the Commercial Appeal. He wasn't in, but dispatch said they would have him call – I never got that call.

The address for Kathy Ledbetter was 1227 Brianwood Cove in Milan, Tennessee. The drive took less than half an hour, and she met me on her porch with fresh coffee.

I estimated Kathy to be in her early 50's. The home was nice, but modest – nothing fancy. Sam was at work, so our only company was Tiger her cat. There was a later model Buick parked in the driveway, and what appeared to be an old work truck parked in the back yard. Nothing here seemed to indicate embezzlement or a misuse of money. These were just plain ordinary folks, living in a plain ordinary small west Tennessee town.

With our coffee and Tiger, we settled in the front porch swing and Kathy began to tell her story. It was the same one Jack had told me. She knew nothing of any missing money, and was alarmed when GMAC stormed in with an audit. Kathy said that Charles and

Carlon were also VERY alarmed when the audit was called, and spent many hours behind closed doors talking with the auditors and among themselves.

"Kathy, tell me about Charles and Carlon. What do you know about them outside the workplace?" I asked when she finished.

"Mr. Reno, I don't know a lot about them – really. Up until 6 months ago a son-in-law – Campbell Miller, basically ran the business. He was my boss, and totally responsible for day to day activities at the main dealership and satellite lots in Dyer and Jackson."

"What happened to Campbell Miller 6 months ago?" Now I had another player.

"Early one morning Mr. Carlon Bosley came into my office and said that Campbell was no longer associated with the dealership, and that I would now be working for him. I never saw or heard from Campbell again. I never saw his name on any documents or any part of the business after that day – which seemed odd, based upon what I had heard."

"What do you mean?"

"A few weeks after Campbell left, I casually asked one of the salesmen if they knew what had happened to him. He told me that Campbell was in the Cayman Islands working on a satellite dealership for Bosley Buick. Now, first that sounded real stupid, and second, if he were still associated with Bosley Buick his name should appear somewhere on some documents...right? I mean no payroll, no expense payments – nothing."

"Did you ever discuss this with Carlon or Charles?" This was getting better by the minute.

"Never got the chance. I came in one morning and found a funeral reef hanging on the showroom door – along with an announcement of Campbell Miller's death. It seems he had been killed in an automobile accident while traveling out of the country. Carlon and Charles had already left to make arrangements for the body, and were not expected to return for several days."

"Weird," I mumbled to myself.

"It gets worse," she nodded. "Two days after Carlon and Charles return, the audit is called. Two weeks after the audit, Leroy Epsee and two deputies show up at my door and arrest me for embezzlement. I knew Jack Logan from my niece who lives in Memphis – I contacted him and here we are today."

"Tell me about Carlon and Charles – personally. What do you know about their family, lifestyle, habits etc.?"

"Both divorced. Actually I think Charles was a widow, his wife had died years ago. They both live well, and I'm sure run in circles that Sam and I have never even thought of. Campbell Miller had been married to Charles's daughter – Annette. However they had divorced several years ago and, as I understand, she remarried. Oddly, I never met her – seems even more odd now that I think of it. Anyway, both Carlon and Charles are men about town and men about West Tennessee. Rich bachelors attract a lot of attention – especially from women who want to be rich without having to earn it. If you know what I mean."

"I do know what you mean. Were there any women in particular that you remember?"

"Not really. They were both always involved with activities surrounding the West Tennessee Strawberry Festival – usually with some former beauty queen driving around in one of their Bosley Buick convertibles. I do recall the name Stephanie Malone being linked to Carlon. She was a former Strawberry Queen, a Miss Something, and who knows what else. Never met her, just photos in the paper."

We had finished the coffee and were wrapping up our conversation when a bright yellow 62 Buick pulled up in front of the house.

Out stepped a man I knew to be a car salesman – I promise I could spot them in any crowd. Short sleeved white shirt with a thin tie and tie clip. Dark colored pants that were too long, didn't fit well and an oversized wallet in the back pocket. Cigarettes in the shirt pocket, along with a couple of ink pens and business cards. They all looked just alike.

He walked to the porch and she introduced me to Jordan Bailey, a salesman with Bosley Buick. Apparently he had stopped by to see how she was doing.

"I hope you're here to help Kathy, "he said as we shook hands. "We go way back to high school, and I am just sick that anyone would ever think she could do something like this."

1962 Buick

"Mr. Bailey, we're certainly going to try and help. I have told Kathy, and I can tell you, I don't think she has anything to worry about."

I said my good-byes and promised to call Kathy before I returned to Memphis. This lady was no embezzler – I would bet my favorite hat on it. Although I had not met Sam, I would imagine him to be a mirror of what I found with Kathy. Something was really wrong here, and I didn't think it was going to take long to find out what it was.

~

I had time to drop by Mom and Dad's house before lunch, and was hurriedly headed that way when I spotted that yellow Buick following me. At Gibson, I pulled off the highway and parked in front of the tomato packing sheds next to the railroad tracks. The Buick pulled up next to me; Jordan Bailey got out and walked up to my car.

I spoke first. "Mr. Bailey, if you wanted to talk further, we could have talked at Kathy's. You didn't need to follow me."

"Yes I did. But, I don't want anyone to know we talked."

"Who is anyone?" I asked, still sitting in my car.

"Never mind – just listen and don't ask me questions. Okay?" He sounded serious; a much different person than I had met at Kathy's only a few minutes earlier.

"No – it's not okay. You can talk and I'll listen. But asking questions is what I do. So...you talk, but keep that in mind."

"Kathy had nothing to do with the missing money – that will come out real soon. The problem is that I know Carlon and Charles have their bags packed, and probably won't be around when it does."

"Oh really? Where are they going?" I was now asking questions.

"I said no questions. I can only speculate on where they're going...the Cayman Islands would be my guess. They've moved a lot of money there over the past few years, and it looks like this program in Milan is coming to an end – soon. Campbell had been down there putting things together when he had his accident – if it was an accident. Carlon and Charles aren't smart enough to keep the business floating, which is why everything has gone downhill so quickly. So, work fast Mr. Detective – you don't have much time."

"What really happened to Campbell Miller?" I was trying.

"I said no questions. Have a safe drive back to Humboldt, and please help Kathy. She and Sam are innocent," he said as he was walking back toward his car.

Jordan Baily got back in his yellow Buick and headed out onto the Milan highway. I put the Ford back on Hwy 70 and pointed it toward Mom and Dad's house.

~

$\mathcal{M}$other was full of news about everything that I really didn't need to know. Dad brought me up to date on his job with the TVA and I managed to keep the visit to less than an hour.

I used their phone to call Leroy Epsee again and invite him to lunch. Scotty Perry answered this time, and said he could reach him on the radio. I asked Scotty to have Leroy meet me at the 'Ramble Inn' – he agreed.

$\mathcal{M}$y order of iced tea and small salad had just arrived when I saw Leroy's cruiser pull into the parking lot. By the time he finally got to my booth, I had already finished the salad – it must be an election year! He spoke and said hello to everyone in the restaurant, before finally pointing himself toward me.

"I don't count? I'm a voter too." I snapped, when he finally sat down in my booth.

"Not in this county. And if you try to vote here, I'll arrest you. Now, to what great favor do we owe this visit by Detective Carson Reno? Wait, I know. You're here for the big party tonight – right?"

"Well, sorta. I'm also working on something for Jack. He's defending Kathy and Sam Ledbetter. You familiar?"

"I should be – I arrested her, but only because the judge made me do it. It simply makes no sense and everyone knows it. That lady and her husband have never stolen anything – I'll stake my job on that." He was as serious as I had ever seen him.

I told him about my visit with Kathy and my subsequent conversation with Jordan Bailey. I then backtracked and told him about my conversations in Bemis, and my search for Alfred E. Dollar.

He didn't seem pleased. "Carson, you're an idiot. Those guys play rough, and I know you know what that means. You could get hurt – permanently."

"I know, but I've got an idea on how we can catch several rats with one big trap. Do you work well with the Madison County Sheriff?"

"Sure. What do you have in mind?"

I told him my plan. He listened, and just kept shaking his head and saying, "you're going to get hurt."

"Leroy, I understand your concern. Let me put the first part in place and see how fast the rats run. We can adjust if it doesn't go as planned," I argued.

"Okay, Carson. But no guns and no rough stuff. Agree?"

"Agreed. Will I see you at the party tonight?"

"Sure, if you look out on the highway for traffic control. Chief of Police, Raymond Griggs, and I have every man available to control this mad affair. We've got the governor and lord knows who else flying into town – it will be one crazy evening."

"Leroy, I would prefer to stay home myself, but I think I do owe it to Mary Ellen to show up."

"Sure you do. And I don't suppose you'll be seeing that Elizabeth Teague at the party – will you?" he grinned.

"Well... she might be there – not sure," I shrugged.

"You're a liar Carson. Now I have to go. You're staying at Chief's, I assume?"

"Yep – call me there if anything happens."

"No, you call and stay in touch with me or one of my deputies if anything happens. And thanks for lunch."

"You didn't eat anything!" I shouted.

"I know," he chuckled before walking out the front door of the 'Ramble Inn'.

~

I had forgotten to ask Leroy about the license number on the car driven by the mysterious Brad Knuchols, so I headed to the sheriff's office to make my request.

Gibson County
SHERIFF'S DEPARTMENT

Jeff Cole was manning the desk.

"Jeff – I need a favor," I asked when he looked up from his paperwork. "Can you run a DMV check on a Memphis tag for me?"

"Sure, but it'll take a while – I know you won't want to wait. Anything about the vehicle we need to know?"

"I'll be able to tell you that when you get me the detail. It may be nothing, but I have a hunch what we learn might be interesting. Its Tennessee tag number 1-4J745."

"Memphis or Shelby County for sure," he seemed curious as he wrote the number on a nearby pad.

"Yep. I'm headed to the party tonight, so if you find out before you leave to direct traffic, call me at Chief's, okay?"

I didn't intend to embarrass him, but he took it that way.

"You know Carson; we have much better things to do than direct traffic so some rich assholes can have a party. Unfortunately,

76

the guest list is so heavy that if we weren't visible, Leroy would never hear the end of it."

"Jeff – I know. And, frankly, I'm glad you guys are going to be around – I just wish I were going to be somewhere else."

"Sure you do Carson. Sure you do," he said returning to his paperwork.

I had time for an afternoon drink before putting on my penguin suit, and Chief's wasn't particularly crowded for a Friday. The jukebox was at its usual volume, and the small TV behind the bar was on mute – as always. Nickie brought me a Jack/Coke, and I watched some silenced Memphis TV reporter standing in front of what appeared to be a burned building or a house trailer and a car. I couldn't read her lips, and I really wasn't interested.

What I was interested in was the group of ladies sitting in the corner booth. They were drinking some of Nickie's cheap wine and completely engrossed in their conversations and themselves. They looked good, and I was thinking, perhaps a beauty review might break out in Chief's – all we needed were judges and some different music!

"Hey Nickie," I said loud enough for her to hear, and hopefully, no one else. "Who's in the beauty review over in the corner?"

"I don't know the names, but they're all former Strawberry Queens or Miss Something or Other. Here for the party, I'm sure. Hey, I have a message for you."

"What? Why didn't you tell me?"

"You don't pay me to take messages – although I wish you did. Your lawyer – Jack Logan called and said he would see you at the party. Guess he had a last minute invitation. That was the message."

"Okay – thanks." I guess Judy Strong had invited Jack to the party – which was a good thing.

It was shaping up for quite a show. I headed off to Cottage 4 for my shower, shave and penguin suit. No cars in front of Cottage 5 – maybe they had already left for the party.

The Party

$\mathcal{T}$he geography was perfect. Humboldt airport was located just across the highway from the Humboldt County Club, and the Mary Ellen Maxwell house was situated less than a quarter mile from the runway. The logistics were also perfect. Caddies from the club drove golf carts, shuffling people from the airport to the club, to the Maxwell house and to/from the parking areas. Parking was either at the Country Club, at the Maxwell home or in a large parking area in a field just off Warmath Circle. I chose the field.

Humboldt Airport

The Humboldt airport was small – very small. Aircraft operation after dark required pre-arrangement and payment upon use – mostly using the honor system. Nickie's cousin, Ted Blaylock, ran the airport, and according to her, he had been contracted to keep airport operations open all weekend. It was apparent many guests would be flying in for the party. This was shaping up to be quite an event.

Governor's Plane

I'm not sure if I was early, late or right on time. I had just gotten the Ford settled in the parking area, when a young man in a golf cart quickly picked me up and headed for the Maxwell residence. Passing the airport, he pointed out Governor Buford Ellington's plane, which had arrived earlier. It brought 8 passengers, including guests and security.

Based upon its size, I'm sure it was one of the larger airplanes to ever use 'Humboldt International Airport'. Yes sir - this was going to be one big event.

I spotted Jeff Cole at the end of the driveway, and asked the cart driver to drop me off with Jeff – I would walk from there.

"Jeff, did you get a make on that tag number?"

"Oh, Hi Carson," he said glancing at me. "Yes, I did. Walk over here to my cruiser; I've got it written down on my pad."

His cruiser was parked in the middle of Warmath Circle with all lights flashing. Jeff was assigned to keep vehicle traffic away from the house and direct them to parking areas in the field or at the Club.

"So who's parked at the house?" I asked when we reached his car.

"Just a select few, mostly family and some overnight guests."

"Guess I didn't make the cut – huh?"

"Well, your name isn't on the list – I can tell you that." He reached into the cruiser and pulled out a note pad. "Here's what DMV had on the tag number. The vehicle is a Dark Blue 1961 Chrysler. It's registered to C&R Distributors with an address on Beale Street – Shelby County, Tennessee. Does that mean anything to you?"

"I'm not sure, but I have some ideas. What I would really like to do is match it up with a Cadillac Limo – but I never got that tag number."

Jeff was interested and ready to help. "We have several limos and they're all parked at the Club. Tell you what – I'll get their tag numbers tonight, and tomorrow see if we have a match. That work?"

"Absolutely...and if you can find out who's riding in that limo, I'll buy you a case of beer and provide myself to help drink it."

"You keep the beer," he chuckled. "Once everyone gets settled, this is going to be a long and slow night – so I'll have plenty of time to check it out. And if we've got some 'bad guys' at our party, I know Sheriff Epsee is going to want to know about it. Catch up with me tomorrow and I'll tell you what I find out."

I headed down the driveway, and then walked toward the main house. Although not dark yet, they had lights everywhere – which meant plans included late night activities. A small band had set-up around the pool, and they were playing soft music as guests mingled, ate, drank, socialized and talked. I counted two bars, with bartenders, around the pool and another in the yard area next to the lake – all crowded. Finger food tables with ice carvings adjoined each bar, and I figured maybe to eat something tonight besides a hamburger.

The main residence door was open, and I could see guests coming and going through that entrance - as well as the pool door, which exited from the den area. I entered the main door. It opened into a large foyer located between the den and formal living room. Sitting in the middle of the foyer was a large white fountain containing a statue of a young naked man standing on one leg. The young man was relieving himself into the contents of the circulating fountain – which was constantly being replenished with champagne by two lovely young female attendants. This was not

here on my last visit and certainly not a part of the normal furnishing – it had to be part of the catering service.

The fountain was drawing a lot of attention, and a lot of use. I'm staring and trying to figure what I was looking at, when a very attractive attendant walked up to where I was standing. "Welcome to the Maxwell home," she said filling a glass and handing it to me.

I'm STILL staring at the fountain when someone threw her arms around me from behind – it was Judy Strong.

"My favorite detective," she said before giving me a kiss and a big hug with an ear nibble. "I am so glad to see you again and thank you for coming. I know Mary Ellen wants to see you, and I suspect her shadow does too."

"Shadow?" I knew what she meant, but had to play dumb.

"Elizabeth Teague – Liz. And don't pretend you don't know what I am talking about. Anyway, Jack is here – somewhere – I seem to have lost him. But I have you, Jack and me a table reserved at the club so we can catch-up during dinner. That okay?"

"Absolutely. Where is Mary Ellen? I would like to say hi and thank her for the invitation."

"Stay right here and watch that lovely little fellow tinkle the champagne – I'll go find her and be back in a jiffy," she said before scurrying off to find Mary Ellen.

With that, she disappeared into the crowd, and I had the little fellow freshen up my glass while I waited.

I didn't know any of these people and assumed they didn't know me either. I was certain that if they DID know me; I was totally unrecognizable in this tuxedo. My instinct and training did have me scanning the room - trying to figure who some of the notables might be. I thought I had spotted the Governor, when Judy came back with Mary Ellen in tow. Only a few steps behind Mary Ellen was Gerald Wayne, of Wayne Manufacturing. I was glad to see they had gotten together – I figured this was a good match for both.

"Carson, thank you so much for coming. It's great to see you again and even nicer to see you under these much better circumstances," she said as I was getting her standard hug and cheek kiss.

Then I spoke to Mr. Wayne, "Good to see you Mr. Wayne. How are you?" I was shaking his hand.

"I am as well as can be expected. Thanks to Mary Ellen, things have been much easier than I anticipated – I guess we owe you thanks for that too."

"You do not. I'm just glad to see everyone moving along and forward with their lives. How is Carrie Mae?"

"She's as great as ever. I'll tell her you said hi, and please stop by to see her while you are in town."

"Will do," I smiled.

Conversation had stopped, and just as I was going to ask Mary Ellen a question she said, "Carson - Liz isn't here yet. She's running late, but is on her way. Her message was for me to look after you until she got here – guess she'll take over then!"

I had no comeback for that comment.

I followed them as they mingled through the crowd, occasionally stopping for some finger food or a fresh glass of champagne. Mary Ellen introduced me to a lot of people, including both her sons – Lewis and Chuck. Two handsome boys that I estimated to be very close in age. The party occasion was Lewis' 21 birthday, she repeated that several times.

Introductions to numerous other nameless people did, at least, have me headed in the right direction – toward one of the bars. Champagne is not my drink – bubbles give me a morning headache.

It was during one of these introductions that I spotted her. The scene reminded me of a queen bee at the hive and 'in heat' - with the male bees constantly circling. She was sitting in a corner next to the open patio doors – just where people traffic would be the heaviest. Men would stop, talk, shake hands then walk off – only to return again a minute or two later. She seemed to greet each one with the same grace and charm – I doubt if she knew any of them or cared, but she certainly had their attention.

As I got closer, I understood the reason for the activity.

It is difficult to define beauty. While everyone recognizes it, they seem to have their own definition of what beauty is. Those are personal definitions from the individual, and if you analyze them they're all the same. I challenge that this lady could be the sum total of all those definitions.

She was modestly dressed, when compared to most other women at the party. That was a message in itself – regardless of what she wore, her beauty overshadowed everything. Flowing blonde hair, flawless features, skin, and lips that glowed with just the right tone – along with the ability to carry all these in the proper manner.

Unlike what you expect from most women, I never heard her speak. She would just nod, bow and shake hands. While her voice probably matched what you saw, she was smart enough to understand that words were not important – she wanted them to look at her, not engage in a conversation.

I didn't know this woman, and I didn't want to know her. My professional instinct told me that the further away I was from this woman, the safer I would be. Unfortunately, I, like many others, was simply overwhelmed with the beauty, and I rudely stared at her – enjoying the flavor to my eyes.

Arms around my waist and an ear nibble brought me back from paradise – it was Liz.

Embarrassed by my staring at this lady, I tried to cover up quickly. "Hey beautiful, I'm trying to pick up a woman – you got any suggestions?"

She gave me a wet kiss and said, "Well, Mr. Reno... looks like you have already made your choice. Do I still stand a chance?"

"Just looking at the candy – I haven't unwrapped anything yet."

"Close your mouth Carson, that's one piece of candy you don't want to unwrap – trust me."

I believed her.

We made it to the bar, had a real drink and then a slow dance to the music from the pool band. It was comfortable to have Liz here. I felt much better.

The next excitement was the arrival of Phillip Chaney. He, evidently, was the rich boyfriend of Charlotte Luckey and his plane had just landed. Announcement was made that he would join everyone, including Charlotte, at the Club reception.

Eventually, we linked with Jack and Judy to make our golf cart trip over to the Country Club. If you can imagine, it was even crazier at the Club. The downstairs bar was overwhelmed, and the only solution was to find our assigned table and begin our drinking operations from there.

Downstairs Bar

Our table was a good one, not too close to the band and not too close to the dance floor. Dinner was served quickly, and Charlie

Rich provided us with a few tunes before Mary Ellen delivered her formal welcome and birthday wishes to her son.

After her welcome, we were on our own – left to our own devices. And using her devices, Liz had a lot of social networking to get accomplished. She quickly left the table to make her 'rounds'. That left Judy, Jack and I to catch up and spend most of the evening discussing other guests.

Judy told me that the attendance guest list was open. That meant key people were able to invite guests of their choosing. I was still looking for Mr. Knuchols – he was probably in the downstairs bar.

The 'beauty' I had spotted earlier at Mary Ellen's was dancing with a very handsome young man – who I assumed to be Phillip Chaney. They made a lovely couple, and I asked Judy what she knew about our 'beauty' and her escort.

"Is this a personal question or a professional one?" she asked with a frown.

"Neither, just curiosity – I promise."

"Carson, in her case, curiosity has killed more than one cat," her story began.

Charlotte Luckey had been the Strawberry Hostess Princess her junior year. Sometime later that year she evidently became the victim of a stalker – originally a rumor, but it eventually became news. With photos, television and constant publicity, her picture was either in the paper or she was making a personal appearance. This stalker became obsessed with Charlotte, and things began to get ugly. He would call her repeatedly at home and sometimes at school. According to the story, he knew her every move – where she went, whom she was with, whom she talked to and even where she had lunch. It was a nightmare. Of course she had done nothing but enter and win a beauty contest – it wasn't her fault that she was a pretty girl.

The local and state police were involved in the investigation, and they eventually had her phone tapped – unfortunately he was making the calls from a payphone not a residence. They made the trace just once and found an empty phone booth with the phone dangling – police had just missed him. Because he seemed to know everything, the police thought it might be a fellow student – someone who could watch and not make her suspicious. It made sense.

Later that year Charlotte and family moved to Trenton and a different school for her, hoping the harassment and stalking would stop – it didn't. When he eventually threatened to kill her, she agreed to a meeting – set up by the police. They caught him. It wasn't a student; in fact, it wasn't even a Humboldt resident. Just some weirdo that lived in Milan – alone. News reports said his house was wallpapered with clippings and photos of Charlotte. Most everyone believes that he would have eventually carried through on his threat to kill her.

Obviously she was one frightened and frustrated young girl. I can't imagine someone her age having to go through that – and all because she won a beauty contest. That's sad.

However, it didn't seem to leave a permanent scar, because she quickly got back into the beauty review business, and was crowned Miss Peabody her senior year.

With her title of Miss Peabody, she entered the Strawberry Festival contest. She was a definite favorite, if not a 'sure thing' to win Strawberry Queen – when the worst happened. Just prior to the Strawberry Festival, a rumor surfaced about her having an affair with a high school teacher. Not just any high school teacher – but the high school football coach, James 'Jimmy' Gannon.

From that point it got uglier. Charlotte was forced to withdraw from the Strawberry Queen competition and Coach Gannon resigned. Fallout continued. James Gannon's wife, Barbara Gannon, sued for divorce and named Charlotte as the reason. Coach Gannon was arrested for having sex with a minor – and he went to jail. Lucky for him, no one would testify and the stink eventually went away – as much as it could. The case never made it to court, and everyone tried to forget the scandal.

After that Charlotte left town, moved to Memphis, and tried to put her life back together – without much success. Back in Humboldt her mother, Loretta, had several run-ins with Barbara Gannon – many involving the police. She blamed Coach Gannon for ruining Charlotte's career and Barbara blamed Charlotte for ruining their marriage. Everybody sued everybody, and eventually it was just absorbed into the woodwork. Barbara took up with some truck driver named Lee Stevens - he briefly tried to resurrect the issue, but now they seem to be settled, and operate a bait shop near Humboldt Lake.

Her mother, Loretta, divorced Charlotte's father, Travis, and married Curtis Turner. Curtis and his family had operated a successful electrical/plumbing business in Humboldt for years until Curtis' gambling got in the way. Evidently he bet and lost on a regular basis – they lost everything and that eventually forced Loretta back to her hairdresser business in Humboldt.

Charlotte had left many in their ruins and they continued to fall. She even had a brief fling with Chuck Maxwell, Mary Ellen's oldest son. But that didn't seem to go anywhere – much to Mary Ellen's delight. Charlotte's high school boyfriend, Billy Vickers, followed her to Memphis – but that didn't work either. She had, somehow, used part of the Vickers family farm money to enroll in Memphis State University. While in college, she met Phillip Chaney, and Charlotte was again moving in the direction she wanted to go. Phillip, along with his father, Forrest Chaney, are old money in Memphis. In addition to real estate, they control much of the shipping coming into the Port of Memphis.

After spending all his money, Billy Vickers was given his 'by-by', and Charlotte was once again the charm of success.

She had natural beauty, and briefly tried to reenter the beauty arena – attending some training schools in Memphis. However it didn't take long to realize the money was somewhere else. Charlotte is here at the party showing her wares, but mostly showing off her new jewel – Phillip Chaney.

"Judy – that is some story!" I was in shock.

"Yes, and all true – as far as I know. I guess the good part is that she doesn't seem any the worse for her adventures. It's a shame we can't say that about those she ran over while having those adventures!"

"What about this new love – Phillip Chaney?" I asked.

"Difficult to tell," Judy said with a frown. "He's certainly got charm and money – but she seems to destroy everything. I hope they can find happiness together."

Liz finally came around, and we managed to get in a dance before the Governor took over. Never one to miss an opportunity, he used the microphone to thank everyone for being here and said he would appreciate our vote in the next election. After a short dance with his wife, he and his entourage left and headed back to his airplane.

After the Governor's speech Liz was off again, and I decided it was time for some fresh air.

Luckily I can still get Cuban cigars from the tobacco shop in the Peabody - and I just happened to have a fresh Fuente in my pocket. It was time for a smoke.

I headed downstairs to grab a drink from Nuddy and use the bar patio for my cigar. Waiting for my Jack and Coke, I finally spotted Brad Knuchols standing in the corner. He was talking to a couple of people I didn't recognize. One was equal to Brad – 6 foot plus and well built - the other was much smaller with short salt/pepper hair.

"Nuddy," I asked. "You see that big guy in the corner wearing the stripped tux?"

"Sure do Carson, but I've never seen him before."

"Who is he talking to? Do you know them?"

"Just the short guy. His name is Mickey Campbell – local bookie and, supposedly tough guy. I've heard he's tied in pretty tight with the Memphis boys, and I believe it."

I got my drink and made my way through the crowd to the patio. It was a beautiful night – cool and a full moon - bright enough to light up most of the golf course.

I lit my Fuente and was admiring the evening when Mickey Campbell came out the bar door, crossed the deck and walked quickly into the parking lot – he never acknowledged my presence. At the edge of the dimly lit parking area, he met someone who obviously didn't belong at the party – he wasn't dressed for it. I learned later that the person he met was Travis Luckey, Charlotte's father. He and Mickey spoke briefly, and then walked together toward the 18th green, quietly talking.

I was contemplating another drink when I heard their voices get louder. They were out of my sight, and I wasn't able to understand the words – but I did understand the tone, and it was not a good one. Within a minute, Mickey was back on the patio; he walked past me again and reentered the downstairs bar. Brad Knuchols and the other gentleman had not moved during his absence, and were still having a conversation in the corner.

Enjoying my cigar and thinking about what I had just seen, I heard another set of loud voices. I couldn't see anyone, but the voices seemed to be coming from somewhere near the golf cart shed. Straining my ears, I determined the voices to be from a man and a woman, and the conversation was getting louder with each word.

It ended with the man yelling, "You no good bitch." It was loud enough to be heard inside, if the music hadn't been playing. Within an instant, Charlotte ran on to the patio and past me crying. She entered the downstairs bar and headed straight for the women's locker room. A moment later Phillip Chaney walked past me and into the bar – I couldn't see where he went from there.

I found my way back at our table, where Liz had finally settled down, and was having a serious discussion with Jack and Judy. Mary Ellen and Gerald had already left. I encouraged Liz into a couple more dances before she insisted we return to Mary Ellen's for a nightcap. I agreed.

Passing the airport, I noticed a number of planes had already left. However, Phillip Chaney's Cessna was still there – where it had been parked earlier.

Along with Jack and Judy, we joined Gerald and Mary Ellen at a table by the pool.

~

"Mary Ellen, I can honestly say I can't remember when I've had more fun – at least when I was dressed this way! You have hosted a terrific party, and I'm sure you son will remember it forever." I was serious.

"Yes, but maybe for all the wrong reasons," she seemed agitated.

"What happened?" Jack asked as he sat down.

"It's that damn Charlotte Luckey. About an hour ago her ex-boyfriend, Billy Vickers, shows up and demands to talk with Charlotte. I had no idea where she was, and politely asked him to leave – he didn't. My son, Chuck, saw the confrontation and then he got involved. Fortunately no punches were thrown and nothing got broken, but it was headed that way. Gerald had already summoned the deputies, Jeff and Scotty, and luckily they got him out of here before things got worse." You could hear the frustration in her voice.

"Well, guess we missed the excitement – huh?" I said trying to ease the tension, but I wasn't ready for what she said next.

"That's not all. Just after the deputies throw Billy Vickers out, Charlotte shows up and she's a little drunk – no, she's a LOT drunk. She walks up to the table where Nancy Young and Laura Westbrook are sitting and pours a glass of champagne on to their heads – both of them at the same time!"

"Is she still here?" I asked looking around.

"Hell no. If she were, I'd have her arrested. She stormed out the front door and into the night. I have no idea where she went and I really don't care." I believed her.

I looked at Judy and asked, "Who are Nancy Young and Laura Westbrook?"

Liz answered for her. "Two beauty queens. You mean you didn't notice them too?"

"No Liz – I did not. After you arrived, all my attention was directed toward you," I lied.

"That's bull-shit Carson, and you know it." She was kidding – I think.

Judy finally answered. "Both Nancy and Laura were in the Strawberry Queen review – the one Charlotte dropped out of. In fact, Laura was crowned queen that year."

"Interesting," I said to no one.

"Yes it is interesting, but let's please change the subject – can we?" Liz said waiving her empty wineglass at everyone.

She didn't wait for an answer. "Carson, I'm hungry – are you?"

"No, I had a great dinner and plenty of finger food." I immediately realized I had said the wrong thing, and quickly changed my answer. "Well, actually, yes I am hungry. Anyone for breakfast?" I asked everyone.

No one even thought of answering – just Liz. "Yes…me. Carson, you and I are having breakfast at my house and I'm cooking. How do you like your eggs?"

Planes, Trains and Automobiles

*L*iz had to work a noon flight to London, so she dropped me off at my car on her way back to Memphis. The old Ford looked lonely sitting in that field all by herself - I had left her all night. It worked out best to ride with Liz and her Corvette - she didn't like my car anyway.

When I got back to Chief's the breakfast crowd was heavy - this was a Saturday morning in a small town. I waved at Nickie and took a stool at the end of the bar – hoping she had some messages for me.

"Jack and Coke, Mr. Reno?" she asked grinning.

"Tell you what. Just hold that thought and bring me some coffee – I've already had breakfast." I should have known better than to say that.

"Well, you didn't have it in your room, and the maid said no one had used the bed."

"Nickie, do you always keep up with your guests like that – or am I just special?"

She looked over her nose at me. "Yes, you are certainly special, and I am always aware of your coming and going. With you – it is necessary. Lord knows when the sheriff, FBI, Federal Marshals or Wyatt Earp will show up looking for you. We run a tight ship here Mr. Reno, and are always here for our guests – and the police."

I knew she was digging and I wasn't going to roll over.

"Stayed with Mom and Dad last night – seemed a good thing to do," I lied.

"Do you want your coffee in a cup or all over your wrinkled tuxedo? Don't bullshit me; I don't have the time or patience." She seemed a little angry – not like her.

"Okay Nickie, I surrender," I said putting my arm around her shoulder. "You seem out of sorts. What's wrong this morning?"

"Sorry Carson. Ronnie has just taken me over the edge this time – I don't mean to take it out on you."

"Should I ask, or just shut-up?" I was really curious.

"Just shut-up. But I'll tell you anyway. Ronnie has taken most of our savings and invested it in some computer-shit thing called ICBM or IBM or something like that. It's not enough that I have to work my tail off to keep this place running, while he can't keep his dick in his pants. Now he takes our hard-earned money and throws it away on something that will never amount to anything. Who does he think he is – John D Rockefeller? What does he know about computers, and what does he know about stocks and investments? I have threatened to kill him since I found out – it still might happen."

"Nickie, I'm sorry – and sorry I asked. Maybe things will work out." I didn't think so.

"And I'm sorry to burden you with my troubles, but please get me out of jail when I kill him, okay?"

"I'll speak to Jack. Bail for murder is tough – but it seems you might have just cause in this case...right?"

"Right! Now I'll get your coffee. You don't want anything to eat? Oh, yeah – you already ate. Bet I know where!" She seemed to perk up a little.

"I ate at your competition," I said trying to defend myself. "No, just coffee please and any messages that came in yesterday or last night."

She went to get the coffee while I endured the relentless jukebox. 24x7 this thing spat out country music and everybody listened and seemed happy about it. They just kept inserting quarters in the damn thing – and it just kept putting their request in escrow for some other day and time.

"Here's your coffee and message," Nickie said returning a moment later, "you only had one. An Al Dollar called and left a Jackson number 529-9011 – sounds like a pay phone."

"No call from Larry Parker?" I was getting concerned.

"Look, I may not wear a short skirt or do shorthand, but I can take messages and write down phone numbers. No – just the one call – that's it. Sorry."

I decided to leave well enough alone and let Nickie plot Ronnie's murder on her own. I was, however, wondering why Larry had not called. This was not like him.

Leaving my coffee on the bar, I went to the outside payphone and called the Jackson number.

"Murphy's Bar," someone answered.

"Hello, I'm returning a call to Al Dollar. Is he there?"

"Just a minute," they replied in a rough tone.

It was only a few seconds, someone picked up the phone and said, *"Hello this is Al – who's this?"*

"This is Carson. You left a message?"

"No asshole, you left the message – I just called you back. What do you want?" He was playing tough guy.

"I had some cars to talk to you about – but they're no longer available. Would you be interested in discussing another opportunity?" I was hoping he would say yes.

"Maybe...you can come over here and we'll talk. But if you're a cop, you won't be returning home. Your decision."

"Okay, I'll meet you. Where is 'here'?"

"Murphy's Bar – I'll be here all day. Just ask for Al."

I wasn't sure I really wanted to do this. "Okay, I'll see you in a couple of hours – at Murphy's Bar."

He hung up, saying nothing else.

I finished my coffee and headed to the sheriff's office. Leroy was on the phone and Jeff was at the front desk.

"You get any info on that Caddy limo tag?" I asked Jeff when he looked up.

"Sure did. Rented by a Mickey Campbell – and we know all about him. Is he connected to your 61 Chrysler?"

"Absolutely. I just don't know how – yet."

Leroy finished his call and hung up the phone. I sat in one of his comfortable office chairs and told him about my conversation with Alfred E. Dollar and my planned meeting. He was, of course, very concerned.

"I'll handle it, but I need you to keep an eye on Jordan Bailey. I don't think he's involved, but he could be in danger – as well as the whole Bosley family."

"I've got the Milan police department watching the dealership; they'll let me know if the brothers make a move or if Al and his group get rough." I felt good about his answer.

I described the man who met with Mickey last night, and asked if he might know who he was. Leroy just started to laugh.

"Certainly, that was Travis Luckey. I just let him out of jail yesterday. We were holding him on a domestic abuse charge and somebody made his bail."

"Do you know who made his bail?" This was strange.

"Nope, but I suspect it was our friend Mickey. Somebody wired the bail money and sent along a train ticket to Hot Springs, Arkansas. Ain't that weird?"

Yes it was, and getting weirder by the second. "Hot Springs?" I questioned.

"Yeah, maybe he's going for his health – but I doubt it, probably going to the horse track. The ticket takes him from Humboldt through Memphis, Jonesboro, Newport, Little Rock and then Hot Springs. Carson, this guy is a loser with a capital L. His wife left him because he gambled - then she turns around and marries another man almost as bad. Last week we arrested Travis for beating up on his ex-wife and, frankly, to protect him. Her current husband, Curtis Turner, has gambled his life away too, but he would kill Travis if he could get his hands on him. Travis is scheduled back for a preliminary hearing next Friday, but I suspect he won't make it. Good riddance – he's nothing but trouble."

"Wow...okay. That's nothing I need to be involved in – I don't think. Please keep me posted on Jordon Bailey and the Bosley's, if they make a move. I'm headed back to Memphis after my meeting with Mr. Dollar. I'll call you before I leave Jackson with an update."

I left the sheriff's office and headed toward Jackson. I made a point to drive by the Humboldt airport – Phillip Chaney's Cessna was still there – parked in the same spot.

I also noticed a new sign for the airport and one that I hadn't seen last night. I guess Mary Ellen's party had really been good for the flying business around Humboldt!

~

Murphy's Bar

A Sign Above the Bar Reads:

"We're Not Happy Until You're Not Happy"

*A*n uninviting place, but sometimes we must do what we must do.

I don't normally carry a weapon – my grandfather's .38 always rests comfortably in the Ford's glove box. However, on this occasion I thought it prudent to stick it in my waistband – hidden by my jacket.

Walking to the back of Murphy's, I asked the bartender if Al Dollar was around.

"Who wants to know?" he asked giving me a dirty look.

"Tell him Carson is asking for him. And while I'm waiting, get me a Budweiser and a cold glass," I said in a nice voice.

I never got the beer. A big ape grabbed me from behind, and threw me over a back table and into a couple of customers. When I came up, I was looking at a very shiny and very big knife.

"Okay Cop," he said showing me the knife and walking straight at me. "Before I field dress you on this table, you got any last requests?"

"Just one," I said sticking my .38 under his chin. "I want to see Alfred E. Dollar and the sooner the better." He didn't move.

It was my turn to be tough. "Now, since you probably don't have brains - unless you want whatever's in your head under that dirty hair deposited on the ceiling of this smelly bar – drop the knife. I'll count to 3." I heard the knife hit the floor.

"Okay…good boy. Congratulations, you'll live to die another day. Now, are you Alfred E. Dollar, or do I need to look somewhere else?"

A voice from behind me said, "I'm Al Dollar. Put the piece away and let's talk. Sorry about the rough stuff, just taking precautions, we never know. And while I'm on the subject – who the hell are you? Some auto broker or something? I don't know you."

"You don't need to know me. Do you know Joe Brody or Alex Russoti? I asked.

"Sure – who doesn't. They handle the rough stuff for the Memphis crowd – since Bubba and Bobby went big time. Why?" He was calming down – this was working.

"Look, I'm not here to swap resumes. Just understand I represent these guys. Can we move on?"

"Sure, sure. What have you got?" Now he was curious.

"I've got 4 full auto carriers that I need to unload fast. I need somebody to take them and turn them for a healthy share and it needs to happen quick."

"Why the rush?" he hesitated.

"Look, I can't add a lot, but will tell you what I do know. These guys in Milan owe the Memphis crowd some money – some real big money. They are willing to dump these cars to cover the debt – that's what I know. We need someone to take them off our hands and turn them for a share – understand? If you're not interested, maybe you could tell who might be."

"What kind of share?"

"$2,000 apiece and I've got 30 cars – you in?"

I saw him smile. "Hell yes I'm in. When can I get the cars?"

"Soon...tomorrow maybe. These guys are leaving the country in a couple of days and I need to wrap up the loose ends as quickly as possible. Where can I have them delivered?"

He took the bait. "Wait a minute. Milan? Leaving the country? A couple of days? Are these coming from Bosley Buick? Yes, it has to be them. Those bastards owe me money. That ain't happening man. No deal! Get out of this bar before I kill you myself. Those bastards can't do this to me!" He was furious.

He grabbed the big guy and they both ran out of the bar. My plan had worked.

~

I used the payphone outside Murphy's bar to call the Gibson County Sheriff's office. Jeff answered.

"Jeff, this is Carson. I need you to reach Leroy on the radio and give him a message – it's urgent - life or death. Can you do that?"

"Absolutely, he said you might be calling. What's the message?" he asked quickly.

"Just tell him that Al Dollar took the bait, and the fuse is lit. I'm confident he and his muscle are headed to Milan as we speak."

"Okay, will do. Can he reach you at Chief's?"

"No, I'm headed to Memphis, but I'll call back when I can get to a phone."

~

I put the nose of the Ford in the wind and pushed the speed limit on Hwy 70/79 headed back home. It was still early on Saturday afternoon, and I think I could actually smell the *'Starlight Lounge'* as I got closer to Memphis. I was going to easily make happy hour, and I was anxious to quiz Rita about Charlotte Luckey. Not that I was personally interested, but I did think her story was an unusual one.

At the *'Starlight'*, I left the Ford in her usual parking spot and stopped at the phone booth out front.

I called Larry Parker – again. I left an urgent message for him to call me at the *'Starlight Lounge'* or at home as quickly as possible. I was getting concerned – failing to return my calls was not like Larry.

My next call was to the Gibson County Sheriff's office – I needed to catch up on the evening's activities. Scotty answered.

"Hey Scotty, this is Carson. Is Leroy available?"

I heard Scotty put the phone against his chest and then a muffled yell, *"Hey Leroy – the bastard's on the phone. You want to talk to him now, or have him call back?"*

I didn't hear Leroy's reply, but assume it was positive. *"Hang on Carson. He's going to take the call in his office – it's a zoo around here."* That didn't sound good!

In less than a minute Leroy picked up. *"Carson, I'm going to kill you. No, I'm first going to arrest you and 'then' I'm going to kill you."*

"Leroy, what did I do?"

"You set this bomb, you light the fuse and when it goes off we pick up the pieces. And, oh by the way, you're not here to help, and are probably sitting at some nightclub in Memphis – right?"

I was definitely not going to answer that question!

"Okay, tell me what happened." This was going to be good. I've never seen Leroy so mad!

~

$\mathcal{M}$ost of it happened like I expected. However, never underestimate a pissed off bad guy – they usually aren't using good judgement.

Leroy's story was the funniest thing I have ever heard or thought about.

Evidently, Al and his muscle partner had spotted the police watching the dealership when they arrived in Milan, and didn't want to tangle with them.

They either waited for the Milan police to leave on another call, or more than likely, placed a police call themselves to pull the deputies off their stakeout.

Bosley Buick

It was a crowded Saturday afternoon at the dealership; the showroom was full of customers, salesmen, employees, new cars and interested citizens getting an early look at the 63 models. This was definitely a busy day at Bosley Buick – and it was going to get busier!

Bosley Buick Showroom

When the Milan police made their exit, Al made his move.

His `58 Oldsmobile was traveling about 60 miles an hour when he hit the front of the showroom - almost square with the entrance door. Before the showroom cars and carnage stopped him, the Oldsmobile had reached the Customer Service desk, which was located at the rear of the showroom.

Luckily, he hadn't killed anybody with his drive through the showroom – but not because he wasn't trying – and he was far from finished.

Al and his muscle partner exited the Oldsmobile with guns in hand. They first shot Charles Bosley when he came out of his office to see what was going on. He had two serious chest wounds, but was expected to survive. They next shot the shop foreman, who charged them with a wrench in both hands – he was also expected to survive, but may never walk again.

Next, the muscle man kicked down Carlon's office door, where they found him hiding under the desk. They didn't shoot him, but beat him without mercy – his survival status was still in question.

The drive through carnage had ruptured several gas tanks on the Oldsmobile and the showroom cars. By the time the police arrived, several were already fully engulfed in flames – only adding to the damage and danger.

Al and his muscle man surrendered without a fight. However, by that time the whole dealership was ablaze, and the fire department was struggling to keep the fire from spreading to cars parked outside – both customer and dealership owned. According to Leroy, nothing like this had ever been seen or even dreamed of in Gibson County or anywhere else – it was a total disaster!

"Leroy, I am speechless." I really was.

"Carson, you just thank your lucky stars that no innocents got seriously hurt in this fiasco. It could have been much worse – believe me."

"I do believe you," I was laughing, but didn't want Leroy to know. "I had no idea anything like this would happen."

"Yeah, well, you got your wish – all the bad guys are in jail. Both the Bosley Brothers are in the hospital, but have been arrested. Albert E. Dollar is upstairs in my jail and singing like a fresh fed canary. If they live, both the Bosley brothers will be spending most of their remaining days in prison – no doubt. As for Mr. Dollar, he'll probably cut a deal with the DA and get some reduced time – but attempted murder is some hard paint to wash off – we'll see. His idiot accomplice will probably get the worst of it – stupid is as stupid does (where have I heard that?). Anyway, your client will certainly walk, as we both knew she would – so you can cash your check with a clear conscience."

"What about Jordan Bailey?" I was concerned about him too.

"He was run over – by a green station wagon, I think. Hard to tell, everything in the showroom was destroyed by the wreck or the fire. It broke his right leg, and he's got a lot of glass cuts and bruises – but will survive."

"Leroy, what you have told me is good news – I think. Regardless, you've got the bad guys and I can turn my attention to other matters here in Memphis. I'll call you next time I'm in town."

"Carson, please don't. Just please don't come to town – that would be better. I'm not sure I can win an election now, and with you around, I know I'll need to look for another job."

He was kidding – I think. "Take care Leroy," I said hanging up. "Talk with you soon."

~

I hung up the phone laughing and trying to imagine Alfred E. Dollar driving through the front of the showroom, and then shooting up the place. I just wish I could have been there.

~

*A*s always, Rita greeted me at the door. Whether I had been gone an hour, a day, a week or several weeks, her greetings were always the same – just like I had been away for a long time, and she was very glad to see me again.

Business at the *'Starlight Lounge'* was just starting to pick up, so I found myself a table and asked Rita to join me when time permitted. As usual, she made that happen in just a few minutes.

"What's up Carson? How are you and that stewardess getting along?"

"We're still sorting out our laundry, but I wanted to ask you about something else. A few days ago you talked about your beauty school and mentioned a girl named Charlotte Luckey. Remember?"

"Sure, what about her?"

"I met her – last night at the party in Humboldt."

"Oh, good Lord Carson – don't tell me that! That girl is no good. She's got money and men on the brain, and probably in most of her other personal private places. You can do better.– stay away from her."

"Rita, you misunderstand. I just met her...well, I guess I actually didn't meet her. I observed her, would be a better way to put it."

"And?"

"Just tell me what you know."

"Why?"

"Because she's hurt some good friends of mine, not physically or anything serious, but I have a hunch her name and/or activities will be trouble again – soon."

Little did I know just how right I was.

Rita told me, basically, the same story I had heard from Judy – the stalker, beauty reviews, men etc. Rita did know a little more about Phillip Chaney and his family background. They were rich and honest - to her knowledge. Father, Forrest Chaney, was a widower and seemed to have no desire to remarry. Phillip had, and did, fill a role as playboy – but she knew of nothing illegal or remotely dishonest about either of them.

That was good enough for me.

"Have you talked to Monica recently?" I asked.

"Yes, every day. And everyday she asks me about you. She's getting nervous, and I think getting ready to file her divorce papers."

"Rita, do me a favor. Call her this evening and tell her not to do anything until she hears from me. I have a hunch she can walk away from this situation in excellent shape, but she doesn't need to do anything yet. I'll call her tomorrow with an update, but I'm just not up to it tonight. I've had a long day and am outta here when I finish this drink."

Rita got up to leave. "I'll tell her you will call tomorrow – right?"

"Correct, I promise."

~

I made a slow drive back to my apartment – still trying to figure out why I had not heard from Larry Parker.

I stopped in the basement bar – more from habit than anything else. Business at the *'Down Under'* was slow for a Saturday night. Andy didn't have live entertainment tonight, so the crowd was light. I had a short J/C and took the elevator ride home.

Taped on my door was a handwritten message from Larry Parker.

Meet me at Police Headquarters, Memphis City Hall at 8:00 AM Sunday morning.

Urgent,

Larry

City Hall

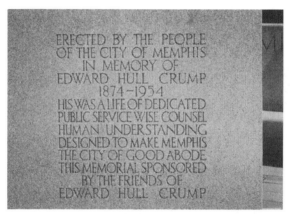

$\mathcal{R}$epeating myself, I am not an early person. Eight o'clock on Sunday morning was not a time I ever knew existed – much less participated in. However, Larry's message was urgent and I knew he was serious – Larry was my friend.

Parking was no problem; the garage was almost empty as was most of the building – I imagined. The desk sergeant directed me to a third floor conference room where I grabbed a cup of stale coffee from a pot in the hallway and knocked on the door.

Larry opened the door and before anyone spoke, I noticed he was not alone. He hurriedly introduced me to Chuck Hutchinson, Memphis Police Chief and Carlton Scruggs, Shelby County Sheriff before inviting me to sit in one of the large padded chairs.

Larry spoke first. "Carson, I have taken the liberty to brief the chief and sheriff on our conversation of last week. And, I'm going to assume you aren't aware of any events that happened while you were out of town."

"Larry, I respect your judgment in sharing information and, no, I am not aware of anything. I've been in Humboldt working on a case and attending a private party with some friends. I did, however, try to call you numerous times, and left a number of messages."

"I know, I got your messages; but considering recent events, I thought it better to talk face to face." He was scaring me.

"Larry, I am all ears. Tell me what's going on."

His story.

On Friday, following our Thursday conversation, he stopped by the Commercial Appeal office to talk with Bernie Taylor. Bernie had not shown up for work and had not called.

Later that afternoon, his office got a call from the Arkansas State Police with an inquiry about Watson Clark. He picked up the message and returned their call. They were looking for information on two former Memphis residents – Watson and Amy Clark. Someone had murdered them both. They had been blown up in a trailer residence belonging to an Amos Duncan – exactly the place I had visited on Wednesday. It was undoubtedly a contract killing, and he believed it was involved with some of the things I had relayed to him during our Thursday lunch conversation.

Because it was in Arkansas, Larry didn't know if anyone in Memphis was aware of my visit to the trailer, but thought it best to not contact me until we could meet in person.

"Wow." Was all I could think of to say.

I sat in silence for a moment waiting on someone to continue with the conversation. When no one spoke I asked, "Well...where are we with an investigation?"

Chief Hutchinson answered. "We are nowhere Mr. Reno. We have some allegations from you that were supposedly communicated to you from a, now, dead man. We know that you were at this Amos Duncan residence, and we know that the bomb was detonated about the same time you were there. We know that the ex-Mayor's wife has hired you to investigate her husband, and we know you witnessed a dinner meeting at The Manhattan Club and claimed it to be mysterious. What we don't know is anything about a secret file, and we don't know if you placed the bomb or if someone followed you and they set the bomb."

That got my hair up. "Wait a minute chief. First, I don't know if anyone followed me or not – but I doubt it. I didn't even know where I was going. I mean...it's possible but very unlikely. And for what reason would I want to kill these people? That makes no sense."

Sheriff Scruggs spoke. "Carson, what we know for sure is that we have two dead people. Two people murdered in a very deliberate and hideous manner. Everything else is just hearsay from you – no facts, no substance, no nothing."

"Okay guys, this interrogation is over. I shared my information with Larry, and truly believe what I heard from Watson Clark and Bernie Taylor to have some merit. My client, Monica Jeffers, is looking for a divorce – that's the sum total of my involvement in this situation. I simply followed instinct. I believe there is more to Barry Lassiter's death than what has been reported and I shared that belief with Larry. Now, you charge me if you have evidence. Otherwise you can reach me in my office – please make an appointment!"

With that said, I got up and left. Pissed would not describe my mood – I was mad.

Larry met me at the elevator. "Carson, go home. I'll meet you at the *'Down Under'* in a couple of hours." He turned around to walk away, and then quickly turned back. "By the way, Leroy Epsee is looking for you."

"Leroy? How did he manage to call you?"

"He didn't. I called him last night looking for you. When we talked, he asked me to have you call him when I located you."

"Okay," was all I could manage to say. I needed to cool down and I guess it would take a Sunday morning Jack Daniel's and Coke to accomplish that.

~

I slowly drove the Ford back to my apartment and tried to analyze what had just happened. Somebody in that room was scared. They were scared of what I might know, or what others might know. I needed to find that missing file and I intended to do just that.

*A*ndy had not yet opened the bar – guess I opened it for him as his first customer. He fixed me a burger for breakfast along with a Jack and Coke to settle my nerves. I settled in to wait for Larry Parker. I trusted Larry and believed, somehow, he had staged that meeting – not sure why, but I figured to find out when he got here.

It was almost noon when Larry perched himself on the stool next to mine. He didn't say anything and ordered a Vodka Tonic from Andy. We both sat in silence for the next five minutes.

"Carson, I know you're pissed. But what I did was necessary."

"Enlighten me," I said.

"Carson, you and I have been friends for a long time. I trust your judgment, and have never questioned your intentions or integrity. However, in this case, you are walking on some very thin ice and against some very heavy political power. This meeting was necessary for two reasons – first to assure your immediate safety and second to let the chief and sheriff know that you weren't just somebody on a witch hunt."

"I figured you had reasons for the meeting, but I never figured 'my safety' to be one of them. You want to explain?"

"These guys play rough, and if what you believe is true, they have some political muscle behind what they do. They wouldn't

112

hesitate to kill you and arrange so that we would never find your body – I believe that. Getting this out to the chief and sheriff was necessary – whether they're involved or not. If they are involved, it isn't likely they would come after you right away. If they aren't involved, then it was important that they know the facts." He was serious.

"Okay, I appreciate that. But, let's me and you get back to a 'me and you' conversation. Can we?" I asked.

"Please let's do."

"Larry, I wasn't followed. Which means the bomb was there while I was there – I was just lucky not to be present when it went off. Which also means that whoever blew up that trailer believes they have destroyed any file or any remaining evidence that Watson may have had."

"Okay. I'll buy that," he said.

"Which brings me back to Bernie Taylor. I believe either Bernie has the file or has some knowledge of where it might be. It wasn't in that trailer – I can tell you that," I nodded.

"I figured that, but I didn't want the people in our meeting to know that. If they're involved then believing the file was destroyed is a good thing. But...we can't find Bernie and that isn't good. He lives alone, and neighbors haven't seen him since Saturday. He hasn't been back to work since talking with you. What does that tell you?"

"It tells me he's scared or maybe dead. If he's alive and knows about the bombing, and he surely does, you may never find him. But, for some reason, I believe that file is hidden somewhere in plain sight. Somewhere no one would think about and somewhere Watson or Bernie couldn't get to. Remember, Watson said he would destroy the file, if he had it. And I can assume from that, he would have had Bernie do the same thing. Make sense?"

"Yes, it does. What are your ideas?"

"I'm going to the Commercial Appeal office tomorrow and ask some questions. That file is somewhere in plain sight, and I'm going to try and find it."

"Okay, Carson, stay in touch. I promise to return your calls, and I suggest you take that gun out of your glove box and keep it handy. Understand?"

I did understand.

He got up to leave and then turned around. "Did you ever call that Gibson County Sheriff, Leroy Epsee?"

"Not yet. Frankly I forgot. I'll do that now. Walk easy Larry, I'll talk with you later."

"I hope so Carson, I hope so." I wish he hadn't put it that way!

~

I went to the pay phone and called Leroy. Oddly enough he was in his office.

"Leroy, Carson here. Larry told me you were looking for me."

"Yes, thanks for calling me back. No big deal, but I wanted to ask you about someone who was at the party Friday night."

"It must be a big deal for you to be in your office on Sunday. Isn't this a day of rest?"

"Sheriffs don't get a day of rest – we're not as privileged as some private detectives I know. Now, do you mind answering my question about the party?"

"Okay, who are you asking about?"

"Charlotte Luckey. Did you see her at the party? Can you add any information?"

"Information...information about what? Yes, I saw her at the party – who didn't? She is pretty hard to miss. You know what I mean?"

"Yes I do. Anyway, her mother started calling here on Saturday saying she never came home after the party. She hasn't stopped calling, and has called almost every hour since then. There isn't much we can do, but I thought I would at least talk with you and see what you might have observed."

"Have you spoken with Mary Ellen?"

"Yes, but I thought I might get your take on what happened?"

"I don't know that anything happened – other than what I'm sure Mary Ellen shared with you. Leroy, this girl is probably shacked up with somebody – most likely that rich boyfriend. She'll come home when she gets good and damn ready. Why waste your time with this?"

"I know, I know – but some things just don't fit. And the mother just keeps insisting something is wrong."

"What doesn't fit?"

"We found Charlotte's car parked at Bailey Park. Strange that it would be there, but we found nothing suspicious in the car. Her boyfriend, Phillip Chaney, flew his plane out on Saturday after spending the night somewhere in Jackson. Now, she could be with him but why leave the car at Bailey Park?"

"Interesting," I mumbled.

"Carson, we're just trying to do our job. I'm sure she'll eventually show up – hangover and all. Then we can all go home and forget about it. But, is there anything from the party that we should know that you haven't already told me?"

"I'm not sure. Let me go over it again with you and you tell me if I left something out."

I again shared with Leroy the events of Friday night surrounding Charlotte Luckey. He listened without asking questions.

"Okay," he said when I finished. *"Everything seems to be in place. I'm going to see if I can locate some others who were at the party and get their story."*

"Good idea and good luck. Do you need me to do anything here – in Memphis?" I asked.

"Nope…just making sure we cover all the bases. I'll call you when she shows up."

I hung up, went back to the bar and got very drunk. I drove the elevator home sometime before midnight.

The Missing File

*F*rom the Peabody parking garage I headed straight for the kitchen. It was early – 11 o'clock. Having an office at the Peabody allowed me to eat in the employee dining room – usually for free. Their large kitchen prepared food for the various hotel restaurants, room service and contracted catering. That meant there was usually food left over, and it was free to employees and tenants.

The bacon, eggs, toast and coffee were a real relief to my aching head. Food, along with a couple of aspirin, almost made me feel like a human being again.

I let Marcie know I was back in town and then quickly went through my mail and messages. There wasn't much interesting. I'd had several calls from Monica, calls from Leroy and a call from Bernie Taylor – which came in Saturday. I assumed it to be a home number, and I returned the call – no answer.

I would call Monica later, but wanted to see what I could learn at the Commercial Appeal before I made that call.

I told Marcie I would be back in an hour and headed over to their office – it was just a short walk.

This was going to be a difficult meeting and I was going to need all my charm, so I took it out and put it on before walking up to the reception desk. My big smile might have been too much, but I needed information, and 'being nice' was the best way to get it.

Greeting me was a pretty, but somehow plain young lady. Her dark hair was pinned to one side with a silly looking clip, and her blouse was buttoned all the way to her chin. Underneath her 'too much' makeup and lipstick, I assumed you would find an aspiring newspaper reporter who has ended up answering the phone and handling visitors. Her nametag read 'Peggy'.

"Hi Peggy, my name is Carson Reno," I said as she looked up from her desk and smiled. I handed her my business card.

"I remember you Mr. Reno – you were here the other day looking for Mr. Watson Clark."

"That's right! I can't believe you remember me. How could you do that? You must see so many people with your job."

"Yes, but you left me your card then too. Remember? See, I still have it." She held up both my cards, and grinned at my silly comment. A very efficient receptionist.

"Peggy, I'm working on a case, and I wonder if you might be able to help me?"

"Is it about Mr. Clark and his wife? About them being murdered?" She seemed sad.

"Yes, it is. Would you like to help?"

"Sure, but what can I do? I just answer the phone, greet visitors and distribute the mail. I really liked Mr. Clark, and would do anything to help – he was a nice man. But, I can't imagine what I could possibly tell you."

"Is there an employee break area or cafeteria where we might talk? Can you get away for 15 or 20 minutes?"

"Sure. Follow that hall and then through the large double doors," she said pointing to an area off to my left. "That's our cafeteria, grab a table and I'll join you in a few minutes. Will that be okay?"

"Certainly," I said nodding with a smile, then walking down the hallway as instructed.

I got some coffee, and was scanning today's paper when Peggy came into the cafeteria. She also got coffee and joined me.

"Peggy, I'm looking for some papers that Watson would have had that he didn't want anybody else to see. Do you have any idea where I could look? Old files, undelivered mail, dead story files – anything?"

"Nope," she said quickly and deliberately. "Whatever there might have been has already been destroyed, reassigned or stolen."

"Stolen? What do you mean stolen?"

"A few weeks ago we had a robbery – which is really strange. This building is always open – we print papers around the clock. But, someone broke into the office area and went through a lot of files – especially those files in Watson's office. After that, the editor reassigned all his work and cleared out his office. There's nothing left."

"No undelivered mail, deal letter files...anything?" I was coming up empty.

"Nothing," she sipped her coffee and thought for a moment. "Well...nothing except maybe that courier who was trying to deliver a registered package. He's been here on several occasions looking for Mr. Clark with a package that requires his signature. When I tell him he no longer works here, he leaves and then returns a day or so later with the same package. Could that mean something?"

"Yes it could! Do you remember the name of the courier service?" Bingo – I had something!

"I believe it was called Chase Courier Service. We use several, but I think that was the name. And Mr. Reno – guess what?"

"What?"

"He was here again on Saturday – the same day we learned about Mr. Clark's murder!'

I thanked Peggy, and promised to let her know what happened. I couldn't get out of there and back to my office fast enough.

Almost running, I entered the Peabody lobby by the Union Avenue East door – I didn't get very far. Standing in front of my office door was Bubba Knight, and that was one person I really did not want to see. I turned around to leave and ran smack into Bobby James.

"Hi Carson, long time no see." He had his hand inside his coat.

"I know Bobby, my apology. I've been meaning to get together with you and Bubba to catch up on old times, but haven't found the chance. Give me a call sometime; we'll have coffee and donuts."

By that time Bubba had joined our little party and I was surrounded – if that's possible.

Bubba spoke. "Carson, is there some place we can talk?"

"Yes – right here in the lobby, and we can watch the ducks. I like public places – don't you?"

Bobby's turn. "Suit yourself. We're here to deliver a message, and we don't deliver messages but once – so listen closely. Up until now you haven't given us any reason to pay you a visit. Up until now you've kept your nose out of our business and tended to your lonely housewives with unfaithful husbands. But word on the street is that you're branching out – that isn't a good idea. If you want to keep doing your little 'marriage counseling' detective business, while still using both legs, you'll put that snooping nose back where it belongs. Am I understood?"

"Bobby – I am so proud of you. When did you learn to put that many words together all at one time? You've been taking night classes – right?"

Bubba's turn. "Carson, that mouth of yours is going to get you in a lot of trouble."

"Bubba, you need to take some lessons from you friend Bobby, he's going back to school to enhance his education. He's able to put more than 10 words together at one time – which is a definite improvement. And speaking of improvement – I understand you guys have been promoted. The B and B boys are steadily moving up the corporate ladder of crime. Congratulations to you both."

Bubba was ready to throw a punch but Bobby stopped him.

Bobby's turn. "Okay, smart ass. You've been warned – and we don't deliver messages twice. Our next visit won't be public, and it won't be nice."

"Thank you guys for stopping by this morning. If you'll let me know ahead of time, I can arrange coffee, or maybe some drinks and snacks. Stop by whenever you're out of jail – we'll do lunch." I was walking away quickly and, happily, still in one piece. They left through the door I had used, and disappeared down Union Ave.

I stopped by Marcie's desk to get the phone book.

"Were those two guys friends of yours?" she frowned.

"No – but why do you ask?"

"They've been hanging around here all morning. I asked to help, but they said they didn't need any help. I didn't like them, they weren't nice."

"Marcie, you are a good judge of character – they are not nice guys."

I took the phone book to my office and quickly looked up the number for *Chase Couriers*. A cordial young female voice answered on the second ring.

"*Chase Couriers – 'we mean business'. This is Theresa speaking – how may I help you?*"

"Theresa, my name is Carson Reno, and you can help me by answering a couple of questions. Can you do that?"

"*I don't know. You'll need to ask the questions first – I'll certainly try,*" she was sincere.

"What happens when you have a certified delivery, with signature required, and you can't deliver that item?"

"*Mr. Reno, it depends on why we can't deliver. If the person refuses to sign, we will return the item to the sender. If the person isn't available, we leave a number for them to call and schedule a delivery. If we make 4 attempts without delivery, we return the item to the sender. Is that what you want to know?*"

"Yes. But, I have another question. What would happen if you were unable to return the item to the original sender?"

"*Well, Mr. Reno – that would be unusual. Why would they not accept the return? After all, it is their item.*"

"Suppose the original sender was dead when you attempted to return the item?"

"Oh my! I don't know. I suppose we would continue to try to deliver to the original receiver...I guess. Actually I really don't know the answer to that question."

"Okay, Theresa. Let's just pretend that did happen. How long would you keep the item, and what would be the disposition? I mean how long would you continue to try to make delivery before doing something else?"

"Undeliverable items are held for claims – assuming the sender, recipient or some legal representative of either party would file a claim. We do send out notices when this happens – but Mr. Reno, we just don't have many circumstances like that."

"Can you tell me if you have a package in claims for a Mr. Watson Clark?"

"No, I cannot do that."

"Can you tell me if you have a package in claims for a Mr. Barry Lassiter?"

"No, Mr. Reno, I cannot do that either. I can't give you any of that information."

"I didn't ask for the package, I just asked if you had one." I was trying.

"I know what you asked, and the answer is still no. We're a licensed confidential courier service. We do not give out the names of any clients or any delivery or receipt information. Sorry."

"Theresa, thank you for your time – I'll be back in touch."

I hung up and thought for a moment, then I called Larry Parker. He was actually in his office.

"Larry, I think I have found the file. But we're going to need a court order to get it."

I explained what I had learned at the Commercial Appeal and what I had learned from Theresa at Chase Courier.

"But you don't even know the package is there?" he argued.

"I know they've been trying to deliver a package to Watson Clark, and I'll bet you a steak dinner that package contains the file we are looking for. They couldn't deliver to Watson, so they tried to return it to Lassiter. Unfortunately, he had already taken a dive off the 100 North Main building. So, they just keep trying to deliver on both ends, with no success. Watson knew this and knew that he would need to return to the Commercial Appeal to get the file. I think he intended to do that, and probably would have destroyed it but the bad guys got to him first. Had they waited, he might be alive and the file wouldn't exist. Ironic, isn't it?"

"What if I visit Chase Courier and see what I can find out? I'll flash the badge around and maybe they'll tell me something. I would be more comfortable going to a judge if I knew the package actually existed. Let me try and I'll call you back. Will you be in your office?"

"Unless Bubba and Bobby come back, then I'm leaving!"

"They came to see you?" There was concern in his voice.

"Yep. They told me my nose was getting in their way. We had cookies and coffee, and they left happy."

"Carson, I told you. Be careful and get that pistol out of your car. I hope you don't need it, but if you do, you'll have it."

"Seems odd. A policeman telling me to arm myself – but okay Larry. I'll do that. Call me after you visit Chase."

Next I called Monica Jeffers. Her maid answered and told me she was in the garden – it would be a minute or two before she got to the phone.

After making my apologies for not calling sooner, I explained that new developments might make my original investigation useless. She didn't understand and I didn't share details. But I asked her to not file any divorce papers until she heard something definite from me. I assured her that this would take no longer than a couple of days, and then I could give her the complete story.

She reluctantly agreed and seemed relieved. Underneath that crust, I believe Monica knew the truth about her husband and his illegal office activities – she just didn't want to admit it.

Ransom

I was busy playing with the mail and anxiously waiting on the return call from Larry, when Marcie buzzed and said I had a visitor.

"Who is it?" I asked.

"His says his name is Phillip Chaney. He claims you two recently met."

I'm not sure we ever really met, but I told her to send him over.

Phillip Chaney was a handsome young man. Tall, muscular, athletic and blond wavy hair – the Troy Donahue look – I call it. He was wearing jeans and a sweatshirt – he looked nervous.

I shook his hand. "Phillip, welcome to my office. I'm not sure we were formally introduced at Mary Ellen's party, but you were certainly pointed out to me by many of her guests. What can I do for you?"

"Mr. Reno, I'm not sure what you can do, and I hope I haven't made a mistake by coming. I heard your name at the party, and they told me you were a private detective and how you had helped Mary Ellen in the past. I guess I'm here now because I need help, and I don't know where else to turn."

Reaching into his back pocket, he retrieved a plain white envelope – which he dropped on my desk. The envelope contained no name, no address and wasn't sealed. Phillip Chaney made himself comfortable in one of my office chairs while I stared at his delivery.

Looking up at him, and without speaking, I slowly opened the envelope and removed its contents. Inside was a single piece of plain white typing paper – neatly folded to fit inside. Unfolding the paper, I saw a poorly typed note using large capital letters. It read:

IF YOU WANT TO SEE CHARLOTTE ALIVE, FOLLOW THESE INSTRUCTIONS.

BRING $200,000 IN SMALL BILLS – TENS AND TWENTIES. RETURN TO HUMBOLDT AND REGISTER AT THE HOLIDAY INN ON HWY 45 IN JACKSON. YOU WILL BE CONTACTED THERE WITH INSTRUCTIONS FOR DELIVERY OF THE MONEY.

IF YOU DON'T BRING THE MONEY – SHE DIES.

IF YOU CONTACT THE POLICE – SHE DIES.

IF YOU INVOLVE ANYONE ELSE – SHE DIES.

THIS IS NO JOKE.

I returned the letter to the envelope, laid it back on my desk and then looked up at Phillip Chaney. He was sitting emotionless, staring at me and waiting on a response.

"Okay, Phillip. Your turn to talk. Tell me where you got this?" I still wasn't sure why he was here.

"It was left on my front porch – taped to the door. I didn't find it until just a few hours ago."

"Have you contacted the police?"

"Absolutely not – can't you read what it says? If I involve the police, they will kill her." He appeared shaken and nervous.

I handed the envelope and note back to him.

"I'm sorry Phillip. I can't help you – or rather I won't help you. I won't help you unless you take this note and your story to the police. Otherwise, I can be of no help to you. You can't negotiate and deal with kidnappers – it never works out...believe me."

"But what am I going to do?" He shouted as he stood up. "I'll happily pay the money, but I don't want to see Charlotte hurt. I couldn't stand it if I did something that got her harmed. I just want to pay the money and set her free."

"Then I suggest you do that. I'll forget this meeting ever happened, and you can handle this yourself. But, I want you to consider this, the chances are good they will take the money and kill her anyway – that's the best reason you need the police involved. They also might just decide to kill you too, and still take the money. If you try to handle this situation yourself, you're not as smart as I think you are. Kidnapping is a federal offense, which means these guys got nothing to lose – once they cross the line there is no crossing back."

I had his attention, but he seemed really scared.

"Phillip, either you take that note and leave or sit down and let's discuss what we need to do. Your decision – and you need to make it now."

He sat down.

"Okay, I'll assume that's your answer and your decision to handle this my way. I'd like to hear you say it – please."

"Yes Mr. Reno. We'll do this your way. Just tell me what to do."

"First, I have some questions. During the party, I overheard you and Charlotte in a spat. She left crying – what was that about?"

"It was about money. She needed money to bail her father out of trouble. He was in deep with gambling debts to some guy named Mickey Campbell, I think. Her father had tried to get money from her mother, and that ended up getting him put in jail. I overreacted when she asked for money, and I wanted to talk it out later – we never did. I promised to talk with her father, but that just seemed to make things worse."

"Did you ever talk with him?"

"No, I never did. And I'm not sure where she went after our fight. I never saw her again that night."

"How did her father contact her? Do you know?" I asked.

"She said he called her the afternoon of the party. I don't know what was said other than he knew we were dating and he knew I had access to money. I assume he was using whatever pressure he could – she never really said."

"Did you know that he was at the club during the party?"

"What? No…no I didn't know," he seemed especially surprised at my question. "You're kidding! Charlotte never said anything about it."

"I'm not sure she knew it either – we would need to ask him or her, but I saw him. I know he was there, and I know he met with Mickey Campbell. That's what I know. Now, where were you Friday night and Saturday?"

He stared and paused before speaking. Either confused by what I had just told him, or searching for the right answer to my question.

"I stayed in Jackson Friday night, and flew the plane back late Saturday. Truth is, I drank too much champagne at the party and that made Saturday a tough day – I had to sober up before flying."

"When did you last see Charlotte?"

"I told you…at the Club when we had our fuss. That's the last time I saw her." He was leaving something out and it was obvious.

"Okay, it seems I'll have to pull information from you. When is the last time you talked to Charlotte?"

"She called me at my hotel room – sometime Friday night, Saturday morning. I'm not sure of the time – I was drunk. Remember?"

Was that a question?

"I remember that's what you told me. Where did she call you from and what did she say?"

"I don't know where she was calling from – probably her house. She didn't say and I didn't ask – I don't think," he was stumbling over words.

"What did she say?" I asked.

"Most of it I don't remember. She just wanted to make up from our fight, said she loved me and would be over to see me the next morning. That's really all I remember."

"No discussions about money or her father?"

"I don't think so, but I was drunk. Remember?"

"Yeah, yeah I remember. When did you learn Charlotte was missing?" I asked.

"I had a message from Sheriff Epsee when I got home Saturday afternoon. I told him what I knew – which was basically nothing and I really wasn't too concerned. Charlotte is the type who would pout when she didn't get what she wanted. I figured that's what she was doing – just pouting."

"Did you tell him about her asking for money?"

"No – it didn't seem relevant, at the time. Guess I should have, huh?"

"Not necessarily, I'm still not sure it's relevant."

"So Mr. Reno – what are we going to do?" he asked.

"What kind of plane do you fly?"

"A 1962 Cessna 172."

"Is it ready to fly?"

"It can be by the time I get to the airport. Why are you asking?"

"How quickly can you get the money together?"

"I can have it ready in an hour," he answered quickly. "But..."

"Geez, that must be nice," I interrupted,"

"What?"

"Never mind. I want you to get the money and yourself to Humboldt this afternoon. Have your limo service take you to the Jackson Holiday Inn and stay there. Do not leave your room for any reason – use room service and don't talk to anybody but me. When you get settled, call my office and give my secretary your room number. Otherwise you are to call no one. Tell your father and family anything but the truth – but do tell them you will not be talking with them for a few days. Inbound calls only, and don't share the room number with anyone other than my secretary. Understand?"

"Yes sir," he answered quietly.

"When Charlotte called you last Friday night, what hotel were you staying at?"

"The Jackson Holiday Inn – the same hotel I'm headed to now. I always stay there when I'm in Jackson."

"Okay. I'll call you when I get settled in Humboldt. Meanwhile, you let me handle the police. When you get delivery instructions, we'll work out our plan then. Until they contact you, there isn't much else we can do but wait. Also, disregard anything you see on the news, I'll tell you anything you need to know. You got all this?"

"Yes sir," he said again.

"Then leave the note with me and get out of here. You need to be in Jackson before dark."

"Yes sir," he said again.

Phillip left, and I sat with my thoughts for a few minutes. Something was wrong with this. I'm not sure what it was, but something just didn't add up. Mickey Campbell and the Memphis Mafia were just too smart to pull this kind of stunt. Without them, that left Travis Luckey to kidnap his own daughter? That made no sense either. Did he contract it out? Was there another player? If so, who?

I was working out my script for the call to Leroy when Marcie called.

"I have Larry Parker on your line two. You still have a client in your office?"

"No, he left. Send me the call."

"*Carson, I'm glad I caught you,*" he said when I picked up the phone.

"Caught me? I've been sitting here on the edge of my chair waiting on your call. Tell me what you found out."

"*I've got good news and bad news – how do you want it?*"

"Quit playing games, Larry. I'll take the bad news first."

"*We found Bernie Taylor.*"

"Shit, Larry, that's good news – right?"

"*No. We found Bernie floating face down in the Wolf River. He'd been there a couple of days, and had a bullet behind his left ear. Does that sound like good news?*"

"Oh no! Certainly that's bad news – I'm sorry to hear that. What's the good news?"

"*Chase Courier has a package with certified delivery to Watson Clark. Barry Lassiter sent the package on the morning of the day he fell of the 100-north Main Building. They won't release the package without a court order, and I'm working on that as we speak. When the judge signs it, I plan on taking the DA with me to retrieve the package.*"

"That is good news."

"*Carson, it's only good news if what we think is in the package is in the package. If it turns out to be somebody's dirty shorts or meaningless correspondence, then we look stupid to everybody.*"

"Good idea taking the DA," I said ignoring his comment. "And you might want to talk to your buddy over at the Federal Marshals office. I'm betting the package is what we think it is, and you're going to need them, if the content says what I think it says."

"*We'll see. I'll call you when I find out. Now Carson, you need to do me a favor.*"

"Sure, what is it?" I asked.

"*Get out of town and get out of town today. Do not pass go and do not collect any money – just leave town. Humboldt will be glad to see you. And don't come back to town until I tell you it's safe. Will you promise me to do that?*"

"Okay, I promise. But please stay in touch. I'll be calling you every few hours until I know what happens."

"You just let me call you. And another thing – don't tell Marcie where you are and don't tell that bartender, Andy either. Don't tell anybody – make up something. Okay?"

I was excited about Larry's information, and would have agreed to anything. "That's a deal. Talk with you soon," I said before hanging up the phone

~

*F*iguring I wouldn't reach him anyway, I decided to head to the apartment and call Leroy from there. Before leaving my office, I told Marcie I was going fishing with some friends in Mississippi. I'm not sure she believed me, but I made it clear that I was not going to Humboldt. A quick visit to the *'Down Under'* for a Jack and Coke to go, and I left the same message with Andy.

Scotty answered when I called for Leroy. He wasn't there, but Scotty said he could reach him on the radio. I let him know it was urgent, and he agreed to radio Leroy and have him call me at my apartment.

I had just finished packing when Leroy called. I told him the entire conversation and story from Phillip Chaney – leaving out nothing.

"Damn you Carson – how do you get yourself involved in things like this?"

I wasn't sure that deserved an answer, but I tried. "Look, I'm just here – they come to me. You should be happy that I convinced him to do the right thing – not something stupid. At least we can try to control what happens – not sit back and hear about it afterwards."

"Carson, there is no WE in that statement. This is a police matter and you will stay out of it. Understand?" Leroy was almost yelling.

"No, I do not understand, and I am already involved – whether you like it or not. I don't want to see anything happen to that girl either. I'm responsible for getting him to involve the police, and you can damn well believe I intend to look after that responsibility. So cut that shit out and let's work together." He knew I was serious.

"Are you coming to Humboldt?"

"Yes, tonight. I'm leaving within the hour. Can we meet early tomorrow? Meet BEFORE you make any attempt to contact Phillip Chaney? Remember, I have the Ransom note."

"Okay, first thing tomorrow. I assume you are staying at Chief's. It might be better to meet there rather than you coming to my office. Anyway, we'll discuss our plans tomorrow and see how you can help. Is that good enough?" Leroy said frankly.

"No, it isn't," I wasn't really satisfied with Leroy's response. "But we'll talk tomorrow. You never mentioned - has anything developed regarding her disappearance?"

"Nothing. She, of course, hasn't shown up – that's basically all we know. I told you we found her car, but nothing suspicious there. Your information brings on a new twist and I really haven't asked anyone else – other family members – if they had been contacted about a ransom. We'll discuss tomorrow. I won't speak to anyone until we talk. Drive careful," Leroy hung up.

I made good time headed to Humboldt - traffic was unusually light.

As always, Chief's was rocking when I arrived and Nickie never saw me walk in. Finding a seat at the end of the bar, I took note of the clients – much different than last week. The 'class' had left and the rednecks had their bar back.

"Well, well, well," Nickie spouted when she spotted me. "Just when we think we have lost the upper class, here they show up again."

"Excuse me Miss Waitress…I'm lost. Could you tell where I might find the Hilton?"

"Listen smart ass I'm not a waitress – I own this place. And I don't know about a Hilton, but we can offer you just as much. That is provided you have your Chief's Frequent Traveler Gold Card. You have one of those?"

"I'm afraid I've misplaced it," I said searching my pockets.

"Then you can have Cabin 4. There's no mini-bar, but it does have clean sheets and warm water – you game?"

"Book it," I said nodding and laughing.

"Carson, what are you doing here? You just left. Oh wait, I know. It's that stewardess – she's pulling on your sensitive parts and you need another yank or two…right?"

"Nickie – I get so excited when you talk dirty!"

"Well, control yourself – it's just talk. You want a drink?"

"Of course, but just a small one." I needed to hit the rack soon. It was going to be a long day tomorrow.

Nickie brought the drink and asked quietly, "Did you hear about that missing girl?"

"Yes, but I doubt that she's missing. Probably just shacked up with some hard tail. She'll show up. That's the kind of person she is."

"Oh really? You know a lot about her?" Nickie spoke much louder.

"No. Just like you, I know what I hear and we all hear the same things. The girl has a lot of excess baggage and that's a shame. She is really one beautiful woman."

"I'll agree with you on both of those points. How long you need the room for?"

"Not sure, but several days. Is that okay?"

"Yes, just let me know, and I almost forgot. Marcie called late this afternoon with a message. She said to tell you Phillip Chaney is in room 317. That's all she said."

"Okay, thanks," I said sipping my drink.

"Who's Phillip Chaney and where is room 317?" she asked.

"Somebody you don't know, and please just forget that information. Okay?"

"What information? See, I already forgot," she was laughing.

"Nickie, I'm going to use that corner booth in the morning. Leroy and I will be having a meeting for maybe an hour or so. Can you try to keep it clear for us?"

"Look, when you roll in here at 11 o'clock, I can make no promises about any table – you know that."

"I'll be in here for breakfast at 8 – promise." I hoped.

"Yes, and I'll probably faint when you do. I'll hold it until 8 o'clock, no longer than that."

"Thanks sweetie. I'll see you for breakfast," I said as she walked away.

I finished my drink and headed for Cottage 4. My plan was for a good night's sleep and a constructive meeting with Sheriff Leroy Epsee in the morning.

Unfortunately the first part didn't work out.

I just couldn't get to sleep. Trying to forget that Bubba and Bobby were probably looking for my head was difficult enough, but trying to figure this missing girl problem was even harder.

Although we'd had our differences over the years, I trusted Leroy and his judgement. I know kidnapping and ransoms weren't the everyday duty of a Gibson County sheriff, but he was smart enough to seek help and use all resources available. However, those resources might get in the way of real investigations – they usually did.

I lay awake for over an hour thinking about that beautiful girl, Charlotte. I was wondering where she might be, and how someone so young could have already had experiences that others wouldn't have in a lifetime. I was also praying that nothing bad had happened.

It was very late on a very warm night when I finally fell asleep. Tomorrow would be a busy day.

Strategy

I thought Nickie would faint when I walked into the restaurant and waved – it was 5 minutes past eight. Leroy was already seated in the booth, and had coffee for both of us.

I ordered biscuits and gravy, and we ate while he briefed me on the Bosley Buick caper. He was still a bit sensitive about the whole thing, but I know it was a big feather in his cap to get these guys behind bars – where they belonged. Alfred E. Dollar would turn states evidence and probably seek a reduced sentence. Jack Logan was already in town and suing for a petition to have all charges against Kathy Ledbetter dropped.

Other than the innocents that were injured at the dealership, I guess things turned out best for everyone. Some bad guys off the streets, some real crooks behind bars and a truly innocent person relieved of criminal charges.

Leroy was happy – even though he was too proud to say so.

"Did you bring the ransom note?" he finally asked.

I gave him the note and he read it – more than twice.

"Okay, Carson, you go first. I would like to hear your thoughts before I give you mine."

"Leroy, something here just doesn't add up. I'm having difficulty trying to understand who would kidnap this girl. Her father? I doubt that. But maybe he hired it done - maybe he hired one of the Memphis Mafia folks to do this. But stand alone, I don't see this as something the boys in Memphis would be involved in, it makes no sense. However, we do know Travis Luckey needs money, so maybe he had somebody snatch her for ransom to pay his debts. That's one idea."

"Any other ideas?" he asked.

"Yes. Maybe there's no kidnapping at all. Maybe Charlotte is staging this whole scenario and hiding away somewhere just to get money from Phillip Chaney. Maybe her mother is somehow involved and helping Charlotte. Maybe her father is working with Charlotte to extort the money.

Or, maybe there really is a kidnapping, and that ex-football coach grabbed her and is trying to put his financial life back together. Or, maybe the ex-boyfriend kidnapped her to recover his family money. Or maybe any combination of the above – all of which seem way out in left field. You agree?"

"I do agree. You have any other ideas?" Leroy asked sipping coffee.

"Yes, but I don't like to think about them," I reluctantly said.

"Carson, I need to hear everything. Remember, you started steering this boat – I need to know where you think it might go."

"Maybe there is no ransom demand. Maybe, for whatever reason, Mr. Phillip Chaney has done away with Charlotte and is using this to cover his crime. Or, maybe Travis Luckey knows she is missing and is trying to make a quick dollar – in that case her missing wouldn't be missing, it would be dead. Regardless, Leroy, any scenario I can come up with that doesn't involve Charlotte trying to get money from Phillip Chaney isn't a good one. Make sense?"

"Unfortunately, Carson, it all makes very good sense. I'm not experienced in handling kidnapping, but this has a different smell to it - I agree. I'm going to call in the FBI and brief them on what we have – I'm not sure what they'll want to do. We'll just have to cooperate and follow their lead."

"How long can you wait before doing that?" I really didn't want the FBI involved, just yet.

"I can't wait – you know the rules."

"Leroy, give me 24 hours. I promise that when Phillip gets money delivery instructions, you can call the FBI. Just lay it all on me – tell them I didn't tell you anything about the ransom note until after he got delivery instruction. But, I agree with you, they must be involved with any ransom delivery. Can you do that?"

"Why, Carson, what's the point? What are you trying to do?"

"I made a promise to Phillip Chaney to not get Charlotte hurt by involving the police, and I want to honor that promise. If the FBI jumps in and she turns up dead, then it becomes our fault. If Phillip Chaney's not involved, then he'll play this through and we let the FBI handle it. If he is involved, then we have him where we want him – it's that simple."

"Let me think on that for a few minutes." I don't believe I had Leroy convinced yet.

"Okay, Leroy, think about this too. If Phillip Chaney is telling the truth, somebody had to be in Memphis to deliver the note - and you told me Travis Luckey didn't have a car. So, unless he found other transportation, or got off the train in Memphis – we definitely have a Memphis connection. Now, while you think about that give me your ideas."

"Carson, I know most of the players. While I don't know much about the Memphis Mafia, I can't rule them out. They want money out of Travis, and probably her step-dad, Curtis Turner too. I think they would go to whatever lengths to get that money – even if that meant kidnapping Charlotte. Regardless of who's responsible, I believe Travis Luckey is somehow involved. I don't know Phillip Chaney, but that's going to change within the next couple of hours. I think I can get a pretty good read, and know if he's sincere and honest about the ransom – but I need to talk with him first. Involvement by the other people is just a crapshoot. They're all capable of pulling some stunt like this – believe me."

"So, what do we do next?" I asked.

"I'm going to give this 24 hours and continue to handle as a missing person case. I'm headed to Jackson to talk with Phillip, and I suggest you call him and tell him I am coming. If nothing happens and he doesn't get money delivery instructions by tomorrow morning, then I will be turning the whole package over to the FBI. I have no choice."

"Fair enough. I'll call Phillip and tell him you're coming. My instructions to him were no outside contact and no outside phone calls – please re-emphasize that to him. He's also to let me - us - know when he's is contacted about a money drop. That okay?"

"Yes, that's okay. What are your plans?" he asked.

"I'm going to see Mrs. Turner, Charlotte's mother, and offer my assistance in looking for her daughter. I'll be interested to see what comes out of that meeting."

~

*W*e finished our coffee, and he left with a promise to talk again after he visited with Phillip Chaney. I headed to the outside payphone.

Phillip answered on the first ring. He said my call was the only call he'd received and he had not made any outgoing calls. I told him Sheriff Leroy Epsee would be over to see him within a couple of hours. He should answer all questions, and cooperate in any way he could. I explained to Phillip that we would be involving the FBI, but not until he received ransom delivery instructions. I told him I would call him back before the end of the day. I headed back into the restaurant to find a phone book.

"Nickie, do you have a phonebook? I need to find an address."

"What's wrong with the one at the outside payphone?"

"You are kidding...right? There hasn't ever been a phonebook with that phone, just that stupid chain hanging where one is supposed to be."

"Carson, don't yell at me, I didn't know. I can't understand why anyone would want to steal a phonebook – they give them away. But if you would use the phone inside, it has a phonebook."

"Nickie, to my knowledge you are the only person that can hear anything on that phone. I don't know which was there first, the phone or the jukebox, but they certainly do not belong together."

Nickie pulled a phonebook from behind the bar. "Here's your phonebook. Who are you trying to find?"

"Curtis and Loretta Turner. You know them?"

"Never heard of them. They local?"

"Somewhere between here and Trenton. Gibson Wells, I think."

Looking in the phonebook, I found the address – Curtis Turner, Rt. 6, Gibson Wells. They had a phone listed, but I decided not to call. I would somehow try to find the house, and then show up unannounced. I liked that plan better.

*T*hirty minutes later I arrived in Gibson Wells, Tennessee. Gibson Wells wasn't really a town, just a couple of old stores located on Hwy 54 – the Trenton/Alamo highway. One building seemed abandoned, and had been without attention for a few years.

But the other showed some signs of life, so I went in to inquire about the Curtis Turner residence.

The nice lady behind the ancient service counter was very helpful, but curious of my questions. I didn't want to volunteer information about the real reason for my visit...so I lied! She reluctantly accepted the story about Mrs. Turner being my mother's hairdresser and she had been unable to contact her by phone. I needed to stop by the Turner home, schedule an appointment for mother and make payment for past services. Bullshit, I know; but sometimes the bigger the tale, the easier it is to sell.

She knew the Turner family well and reluctantly provided directions to their home. She instructed me to drive north on Hwy 54, where I should exit left onto Layman Road. The Turner residence would be about a mile down Layman Road, on the right hand side.

I thanked her for the information, grabbed a soda from her drink box, and then headed toward the Curtis Turner residence.

The house was located just where the lady said it would be, and the mailbox read: Curtis and Loretta Turner, Rt.6, Gibson Wells.

A narrow gravel driveway led from the highway up a slight hill to a modest wood framed home with a large front porch. Despite being weathered with age, and in need of a little paint, the house was in good condition. The yard and landscaping showed evidence of being well cared for, and the home had a certain 'warmness' in appearance. I liked it.

I parked the Ford under a large Oak tree, then remained in the car looking at the house. There were no other vehicles around, so I was surprised when a dark-haired, middle aged woman opened the screen door and stepped out onto the porch. She held the door open and stared at me with a facial expression that said 'who are you?'

As I approached the porch, and got closer to where she was standing, there was no question this lady was Charlotte Luckey's mother. Although wrinkled with age and hardened with miles, she had the same features I had seen in Charlotte. When younger, I'm sure Loretta Luckey had been a very beautiful woman.

She was still holding the screen door and staring when I introduced myself.

"Mrs. Turner? My name is Carson Reno. Sheriff Epsee asked me to drop by. He told me of your trouble, and has asked me to help him, and you in locating Charlotte. Do you have a few minutes?"

She was wearing a faded blue cotton dress surrounded by a kitchen apron that was showing a lot of fresh stains. Her voice was shaky, but pleasant.

"Please call me Loretta. And again, who are you?" she asked.

"My name is Carson Reno. I'm a private detective from Memphis, but I grew up in Humboldt. In fact, my parents still live there. Sheriff Epsee and I are old friends, and since I was in town on another matter, he asked me to see if I could help find your daughter. I thought the best place to start was to talk with you."

"Please come in Mr. Reno, and excuse the way I look. I'm canning butter beans, and I believe I have more on me than I have in the jars. Do you like butter beans Mr. Reno?"

"Call me Carson, and yes, I love butter beans. Did you have a good crop this year?" The aroma from the cooked butter beans was knee deep where I was standing. It was lunchtime, and it reminded me that I hadn't eaten - the smell was making me hungry.

"Oh no. These came from my neighbor down the road. We don't have a garden, and I wouldn't have the time to tend it anyway. I'm a hairdresser by trade and operate 'Loretta's Hair Care' in Humboldt. I'm sure you've seen it – it's next to Baggett's Market on 22nd Avenue."

"Yes, absolutely, I drive by there all the time." I had never seen the place.

I followed her into a well-furnished living room, and she pointed to a large couch that sat in the center of the room. "Please have a seat and excuse the mess. I wasn't expecting company this morning.

Mess? What mess? The room was immaculate and extremely comfortable – like something from a painting. Everything was in its place, even down to the small linen cloths that covered the arms of the couch and chairs.

"I'm sorry to barge in without calling first," I apologized. "But Leroy suggested I come talk with you as soon as possible."

She straightened her apron before sitting down in a small wooden chair across from the couch. "That's okay, and I really should be at work today. But, with Charlotte missing I...I just couldn't..."

She lost her composure for a moment, and used a tissue she had been carrying to dab a small tear. Then her strength showed, and she regained it quickly before speaking. "How can I help you Mr. Reno – I mean Carson?"

"I would like for you to repeat what you've already told the sheriff and allow me to ask a few questions. Will that be okay?"

"Sure, but there isn't very much to tell. She left here last Friday afternoon headed to a party at the Maxwell home. I expected her to be late, but she did say she would be coming home that night. That is the last time I saw my daughter. They found her car at Bailey Park and...and that's all I know."

"Has Charlotte ever done anything like this before? I mean go missing for several days?"

"No sir. If she weren't coming home she would always call and let me know where she was. Mr. Reno – I mean Carson, we talk all the time like a mother and daughter should. Even when she was in college, she would call me most every day. Now she's been gone 4 days and ..." She wasn't able to hold back the tears any longer. "Excuse me Mr. Reno, let me wipe my face – I'll be right back."

She headed off toward the kitchen, and I used the opportunity to look around the large room. As I said, everything was in its place, and despite the open windows and door, not a speck of dust on anything.

Neatly placed around the room was the usual stuff, including several photos, but the photos were only of Charlotte – no other family member in any of the pictures. On the small mantel were a couple of trophies – one reading Miss Peabody and another reading Hostess Princess West Tennessee Strawberry Festival.

Loretta had regained her composure and offered a small smile when she came back in to the living room.

"I'm sorry Mr. Reno, I'm sure you understand."

"Absolutely. Just a couple more questions and I'll leave you alone. How often does Charlotte see her father?"

"Never, I hope. That bastard is worthless. Please excuse my language, but he gambled away everything he or we ever had. He showed up here several days ago needing money, and I had to call the sheriff. He hit me Mr. Reno – he hurt me. I don't want Charlotte around somebody like him which is why we're divorced. Her step dad, Curtis, is nice to her. Unfortunately, he isn't around much – he's a truck driver and is gone most of the time. But he worships Charlotte – I know that much."

"Does your ex-husband, Travis, have a car?"

"Not to my knowledge. He sometimes borrows a car from one of his gambling friends, but he doesn't own one – doesn't own much of anything, I suppose."

"Do you know Phillip Chaney?" I asked.

"Nope, never met him. But Charlotte has sure told me a lot about him – I think she really likes him. I understand he has money and comes from a nice Memphis family. I hope they get together, she needs something good to happen."

"Tell me about Billy Vickers," I asked calmly.

"He's worthless too. His family thought he and Charlotte were going to get married, so they gave her money to go to college – now they want it back. I don't talk to them Mr. Reno, we don't get along."

"I'm going to let you get back to your butter beans," I said standing up. "And I promise to call you when we find out anything on Charlotte's whereabouts. Will that be alright?"

"Yes, please. My number is in the book, and I'm sorry to keep calling you Mr. Reno – I know you said call you Carson. But you are so nice and professional – the Mr. Reno just sounded better to me."

"That's fine. Calling you Mrs. Turner sounded better to me too. I'll be in touch." I stepped toward the door.

"Wait, Mr. Reno. Let me give you some canned butter beans. I'll be right back."

I stood next to the screen door and watched her scurry off toward the back of the house. Within a minute, she came back with a large brown paper bag containing 6 jars of fresh canned butter beans. I was hungry enough to eat them standing in her living room!

"Thank you Mrs. Turner – I can't remember when I last had canned butter beans. Can I ask you one more question?"

"Sure. What is it?" she said turning to face me.

"Do you know if your ex-husband might have a key to Charlotte's car?"

"No idea. He could, I suppose. Why do you ask?"

"I'm not sure, Mrs. Turner. Thank you so much for your information and especially thank you for the canned butter beans. My kitchen will not know how to react. I'll call you with any information."

I headed back to the highway with plans to get to Chief's for lunch. I also was hoping to catch up with Leroy after his talk with Phillip.

I felt sorry for Charlotte's mother, she was such a nice person and it was evident that she loved her daughter very much. I knew it would be rough on her if something had happened to Charlotte, and even rougher if Charlotte's father were involved.

~

The dark blue 61 Chrysler was parked at the Gibson Wells store and it pulled out behind me when I went by. They remained 3 or 4 hundred yards behind – seeming comfortable following and making no effort to stop me.

~

146

*T*he road to and from Gibson Wells and Humboldt takes you through the black neighborhoods of Humboldt – an area known as *'the Crossing'*. The name denotes the point where the north/south Gulf, Mobile & Northern (GM&N) and the east/west Louisville and Nashville (L&N) railroads cross. During the harvest season, the Crossing is where farmers bring their crops to be graded, packed and shipped on railroad cars to various processing plants. While some strawberries are routed this way, the majority of activity is centered on cabbage, corn, melons and tomatoes. Trucks will line up for miles waiting to unload produce at the various packing sheds for grading and packing. These sheds operate around the clock, with the employees working 80 to 100 hours per week. Farmers want to be unloaded quickly and get back to their farms to gather more products. The produce buyers want to make sure fruits and vegetables are rapidly processed and on their way to market as soon as possible. This was harvest season, and the Crossing was bustling with activity. Vehicles lined both sides of the road, and occupied most every available parking area.

Packing Shed – The Crossing

I figured the Chrysler occupants had learned from the storekeeper who I was visiting, and this tail was more of a way to harass me, rather than being interested in my business. I don't like harassment, and I don't like to be followed.

On 9th Street I pulled over and parked in front of the old icehouse. Standing next to my car, I waited for the Chrysler to come by – it only took a minute.

Beare Ice and Coal

The Chrysler slowed when they spotted me standing next to the Ford, and I thought for a moment they were going to drive by. They didn't. Quickly wheeling into the small parking area, the Chrysler pulled up next to my Ford and stopped abruptly. Brad Knuchols was driving and Mickey Campbell was riding shotgun. There were two other men in the back seat – Mafia 'tough guys' I assumed. Mickey got out, lit a cigarette and walked up to where I was standing.

He, just like the others in the car, was dressed in a dark suit with a dark shirt, hat and no tie – all tailor made, I'd bet. A little 'overdressed' for a warm spring day, but being a 'tough guy' did have its drawbacks – I suppose.

"Mr. Reno – I don't think we've had the pleasure. Please allow me to introduce myself, my name is Mickey Campbell." He handed me a business card.

Mickey Campbell, Agent/Owner

Campbell Realty

Bemis, Tennessee
GA9-8046

I looked at his card, then handed it back to him. "Okay – now that you have introduced yourself. You want to tell me why you're following me?" I was not nice.

"Following you? No...no, not at all – Mr. Reno. My associates and I were just checking on some property in the Gibson Wells area when we saw you." Brad Knuchols had gotten out of the car and was leaning against the hood. The other two remained in the back seat.

"Saw me? So you must know who I am. How?" I didn't think I was going to like his answer.

"Yes I, I mean we, do know who you are. We know you are looking into the disappearance of that beauty queen – Charlotte Luckey. An unfortunate situation. Any luck?"

"Frankly, that's none of your business, Mr. Campbell. I don't like being followed and I don't like your conversation or your questions. Now, just tell me what you want, and let's all get on with our business. I'm sure you and your associates have lots of real estate to show and sell today."

"Mr. Reno, my associates – and myself – want you to know that we had nothing to do with the disappearance of this beauty queen. So, as you continue your efforts to try to find her, please make sure you channel those efforts in some other direction – not our way. Understand?"

"Well Mr. Campbell, this is really interesting. You and 'your associates' are in Gibson Wells checking up on this missing girl's mother and stepfather. Then you see me, and know that I have been to visit with them. Now you, and 'your associates', find it necessary to tell me you had nothing to do with her disappearance? Has someone asked you if you were involved, or are you announcing your innocence without being asked?"

He didn't like my question.

"No, and we don't intend to be asked by you, that hick sheriff or anyone else. Just stay out of our business, and look somewhere else for your lost girl. We're sorry she's missing and we hope you find her – but don't stick your nose into our business. It wouldn't be healthy."

"Tell you what – Mr. Campbell. I know you met and talked with her father, Travis Luckey, last Friday at the Country Club. You tell me what that meeting was about, and I'll promise to keep my nose out of your business. Okay?"

Before I finished speaking, Brad Knuchols had walked around the car and positioned himself behind me. Then the other two 'goons' got out of the back seat and walked over.

"Jeez Mr. Campbell, you got enough help? Think you four guys can handle me?" I was hoping they were just showing muscle and not serious.

"Let's leave it at this, Mr. Reno. If you interfere with me or any of my business activities – Mr. Brody and Mr. Russoti will be coming to see you. Have you met Mr. Brody and Mr. Russoti? Should I introduce you?"

"No need. All these grease-balls look and smell alike anyway. Have them wear a name tag, so I can tell them apart." They didn't like that statement, and Brad Knuchols was inching himself closer.

"Mr. Reno, you have a very smart mouth. I just hope you get to keep the teeth that are in it. We'll be leaving now, but please remember our conversation – we are not involved in this young girl's disappearance."

I watched as they all slowly got back into the Chrysler and left. Probably had some big real estate deal waiting.

~

I drove back to Chief's and finally ordered some lunch. Ronnie was offering meat loaf, white beans, corn and a roll – I placed my request with Nickie.

She only had one message – it was from Larry Parker and I returned his call. He was in his office and let me know that the package did contain a file – but he didn't know what was in it. He did say the DA was reviewing the contents and would call back when he had more information.

Back on my barstool, I was thinking about desert when Leroy's cruiser pulled into the parking lot. He opened the front door, waved at some potential voter and joined me at the counter.

"How did your meeting with Phillip Chaney go?" I asked.

"Not good Carson, not good at all. When I got to the Holiday Inn he was gone. I found him and his brother at the Humboldt airport warming up his plane."

"Brother? Where the hell did a brother come from? Nobody has ever mentioned a brother, and he wasn't to see or talk to anybody – including family members. Can't this guy follow simple instructions?"

"His story is that he got the ransom call with instructions, and was following through with those instructions. Didn't he call you?"

"No he did not – I don't think. Nickie, I didn't get a call from Phillip Chaney, did I?" I shouted across the room.

She stared at me hard. "Carson, when you walked in here I gave you your messages – there was just one. Did I give you a message from Phillip Chaney?"

"No, you didn't."

"Then you didn't have a message from Phillip Chaney." She was making me feel bad for asking.

"Leroy, what were the instructions?" I was pissed, or disappointed – not sure which, but probably both.

"He is to fly to the Halls Airstrip and land at four o'clock, taxi to the end of the west runway and leave a briefcase with the money at the end of the airstrip. Then he's to leave. That's it."

"Halls?"

"Yes, not an active airport anymore. They use it for drag racing on weekends, but it is isolated. Makes some sense."

"Is he going?"

"Sure, but not alone – his brother is going with him. It's only a 20-minute flight, so he won't be leaving for a couple of hours. I've contacted the FBI in Jackson, and they have assigned agents Giltner and Raines to handle. I need that ransom note to take to Jackson. The FBI wants to see the note before the drop. They won't be in touch with Chaney, but will be at the airport to apprehend whoever shows to pick up the money."

I handed Leroy the note. "You headed to Jackson now?"

"Yep – you want to tag along?" he asked.

"Yes, let's go."

"Carson, are you sure? These FBI guys are going to question you – be prepared with your answers."

"I've nothing to hide – let's go." I was serious.

We jumped in Leroy's cruiser and sped off toward the FBI office in Jackson. This gave me a chance to share with him my conversation with Loretta Turner and my roadside meeting with Mickey Campbell and his goons.

"What's your take on Mickey Campbell and his crew?" he asked.

"Cheap thugs. I'm no longer convinced they don't have a part in this kidnapping or Charlotte's disappearance – but I don't think it's their doing. However, now they're afraid that all the attention will muddy up their business. Why can't you lock these crooks up?"

"I can't catch them doing anything. We pick up some scraps, but these guys keep themselves above getting busted. They operate over several jurisdictions, and none of us really have the manpower to devote full time personnel toward organized crime activity. The Federal boys need to handle that – but they don't. We'll get them one day – crime doesn't pay forever. Just ask the Bosley brothers!"

"I hope I can be there the next time that happens." We both laughed.

"Carson, one other thing I forgot to tell you – Charlotte's car is missing."

"What does that mean – missing?"

"We examined the car when we found it in Bailey Park and found nothing. So, it was towed to Deloch for storage – it's that simple. Deloch called the office this morning and said the car was missing – guess overnight somebody stole it or took it, for some unknown reason."

"What kind of car does she have?"

"1958 Ford Thunderbird – White. Nice car, but a lot of miles on it."

"I think Travis has that car," I said bluntly

"Travis? Does he have a key?" Leroy was interested.

"I don't know, but if he's played the role I think he has, he needed transportation. Whether he originally parked the car in Bailey Park or not, I think he used the car – maybe to deliver a ransom note in Memphis. Now maybe he needs the car again, who knows? It's just a theory."

"Interesting thought. We'll find the car. You can't hide that car in this county – trust me."

"Maybe it isn't in this county. Maybe it isn't even in this state!"

~

I spent 45 tough minutes with the FBI agents. They came down on me pretty hard about not immediately turning over the note. But underneath their dark suits and thick skin, I think they understood the reasons for my actions.

Regardless, I got off with a lecture and a warning to stay away from Phillip Chaney until this matter was resolved. I promised to do that – even though I had no intentions of doing so.

Leroy and I headed back to Humboldt. "Carson, I could see it in your eyes – you've got something up your sleeve. If you're smart, you won't cross the FBI again – you might end up on the wrong side of a jail door."

"I'm just going to let this thing play itself out first. We'll see what happens. I'll promise to make no moves unless I tell you first. Okay?"

"I guess, but be careful," Leroy answered.

~

*B*ack at Chief's, Nickie had taken two calls for me. One was from Larry Parker and the other from Elizabeth Teague. I called Larry first.

He told me the DA had reviewed the package and only had one comment – WOW! He wasn't sure what that meant, but I think we both knew. He had the goods to make some pretty big heads roll in Memphis and Shelby County Government. This would be fun to watch.

The number Liz left was local, so I knew she must be in town. I called her next.

She answered first ring. *"Hey handsome, you in town to see me?"* Her conversations always put a good spirit on every situation.

"I won't lie – yes I am." I lied.

"Well, I called your apartment and your office. Marcie said you had gone fishing. Did you catch anything? Let me rephrase that – did you catch anything that you can't get rid of without a doctor?"

"No, silly. I'll explain the fishing story later. You available for dinner or maybe a movie?"

"Absolutely. You grab some beer and I'll pick you up at 7. We'll go snuggle at the drive-in movie. Okay?

"It's a date – see you then," I said hanging up the phone.

Confusion

I had a few hours before my date with Liz, so I found a comfortable stool at Nickie's bar and waited for events to unfold.

Ronnie had a small television over the bar, which remained on with the volume turned down. But it didn't matter; you couldn't hear it over the jukebox anyway. I could, at least, get some feeling for what was happening outside Humboldt.

"Nickie, I'll take a Jack and Coke, and could you put that TV on a Memphis channel?" I asked nicely.

"I don't want to give you the wrong impression of our little city, but Memphis channels are all we get," she shot back. "Do you have a special request? I can manage 5 and 13 without sending Ronnie on the roof to adjust our antenna."

"Just put it on a station that I can see. Okay?"

"No problem Mr. Reno. We've got 'Guiding Light' on one and 'As the World Turns' on the other. What's your choice?"

"Channel 5 would be great – if it isn't too much trouble." I was being sarcastic.

At 4:30 the soap opera saga was interrupted by what was labeled a 'Special Report' and the headline 'Breaking News'. I, obviously, couldn't tell what the reporter was saying, but she was standing on the steps of Memphis City Hall and holding some documents for the camera – we'll never know what they were. In a few minutes the District Attorney appeared and made a short statement, after which we were quickly returned to 'As the World Turns'.

No wonder people in this town went crazy – soap operas, game shows and Gun Smoke reruns. News and world events were not something the citizens of Humboldt paid much attention to. I was caught in that maze and would be forced to rely on the phone and newspapers for any news that didn't involve cattle futures, wholesale produce prices, garden club updates or the Strawberry Festival. This was their world and welcome to it.

At 4:45 Leroy called. Nickie took the call.

"Get his number and I'll call him back from the outside payphone," I said to Nickie.

He told her he was in his office, and I immediately called him back.

"Carson, it was a 'no-show' on the ransom pickup. Chaney followed instructions to the letter, but after waiting an hour, the FBI called it and retrieved the payoff money."

"So – what next?" I asked.

"Chaney will wait at the hotel tonight to see if any further contact is made. If not – he'll return to Memphis tomorrow. If he's contacted after that, he will immediately notify the FBI. For him, that's it."

"What else?" There had to be more.

"Agent Giltner is assigned to the case and will be working with my office and the State Police regarding our missing Charlotte Luckey. They're driving the investigation from this point forward. My hands are tied," he sounded discouraged.

"Well, mine aren't, and I'm going to ruffle some feathers. Somebody is either playing me for an idiot or playing us all for idiots – and I've got an idea who that somebody might be." I was serious.

"Carson, be careful. I'll cover your back when I can, just don't make this go somewhere it doesn't need to go. Okay?"

"I think I understand what you mean, but I only want to find that girl and find the truth. I'll keep you in the loop – promise."

I must have had an obvious frown on my face when I walked back into Chief's.

"Bad news?" Nickie asked.

"Bureaucracy. Justice has to open too many doors before it gets delivered."

"What? Is something wrong with your drink?"

"Yes – it's empty. Please get me another."

I didn't have a plan – I just had ideas. Phillip Chaney was hiding something – I didn't know what, but I intended to find out. He had lied to me, and I especially didn't like that. Travis Luckey was involved, but I didn't know how. Somewhere there was a common thread, but there was also a wildcard – I needed to find both the thread and the wildcard. I needed a plan.

~

*W*ith a shower, shave and change of clothes, I wandered back into the bar to wait on Liz.

"Nickie, I'll have one more Jack/Coke, and would you sack me up a six pack of Budweiser? Throw some ice in the sack too, please."

"Wait a minute – what's that smell?" She was sniffing the air as she walked toward me. "I know! It's male hormone! You got it coming out every pore. I first confused it with after-shave, but no, it's definitely male hormone. I have smelled it before – just not recently."

"Nickie, you're funny, but nuts. I have a date, and we're going to the drive-in movie. We are going in a two seat convertible car, so its movie, popcorn and beer – that's all."

"Sure, sure. What's the movie?"

"I have no idea." She had me there.

"So, you're not going for the movie, and I have beer and popcorn here. You do the math."

"Nickie, do you get the Memphis paper?" I asked changing the subject.

"Sure do. We get the morning edition Commercial Appeal. It usually gets here about 2:00 PM."

"Wait a minute. Your morning paper gets here at 2:00 PM? What kind of a morning paper is that?"

"It's the morning paper we get every day – usually around 2:00 PM," she was serious.

"Okay – whatever. Just make sure to save me a copy – please."

"Will do – have fun at the movies." I actually think Nickie was jealous.

Skyway Drive-Inn Theater

*I*t was a great evening for a drive-inn movie. We had the top down on Liz's corvette, the moon was bright, stars were out, weather was cool enough to make you snuggle, we had cold beer and some catching up to do with each other. I have no idea what movie was playing, and it didn't matter because we weren't watching it anyway.

Skyway Drive-Inn Theater is located on Hwy 45N, just outside town. Tuesday night was not normally a busy night for the drive-inn, but ideal weather had brought a number of people out to see the movie and enjoy the evening.

We had talked through most of the feature, and I shared as much detail with Liz as I thought appropriate. I wanted her to understand the situation, but not necessarily the danger that was involved.

We were half way through the beer, and I had just returned with a fresh supply of popcorn when our evening went terribly wrong. A person walking by our car – assumed to be headed to the concession stands – stopped and put a gun barrel in my left ear.

He said, "Please don't say anything, just get out of the car and follow me."

I don't follow instructions well – as you have probably already noted.

I looked at my attacker and chuckled, "Well, hello, Mr. Luckey. Are you not enjoying the movie? Can I offer you a beer?"

"Stop the bullshit Reno. Unless you want yourself or this pretty lady hurt, you'll come with me. Understand?"

"Perfectly...I am your prisoner." I turned to Liz, "Elizabeth, would you please call Mr. Epsee and tell him I'm going to be visiting with Mr. Travis Luckey for the next little while. Tell him I'll call when appropriate."

Of course Liz is upset with my words and starts yelling at Travis as she's starting to get out of the car, "You son-of-a-bitch, you can't do this!" I put my hands up to stop her.

"Liz, it's okay...really. Travis and I are just going to talk. Go find Leroy and tell him what I just told you. Everything will be just fine – trust me."

Leaving a speechless Liz behind, I followed Travis Luckey over to Charlotte's 58 T-Bird and got in the passenger side. We exited the theater and drove south toward town without either of us speaking. At Bailey Park he took the north entrance, and stopped in front of the recreation pavilion.

Then he did something really weird.

He handed me his gun.

"I'm surrendering myself to you, Mr. Reno. These guys are going to kill me, and I simply don't know who to trust."

I thought for a minute. "Let's get out of the car and go over to the playground. This place is going to get busy in a few minutes, and that might give us more time to talk."

We both sat in a swing and he told me his story.

~

*H*e was in deep to Mickey – gambling debts. Mickey had bailed him out of jail because he knew he couldn't repay the debt while sitting in a cell. The train ticket was just a decoy to give him some alibi for what would happen next. According to Travis, everything was Mickey's plan – and he just went along with the idea.

He and Charlotte would plan her disappearance. They were to meet in Bailey Park on that Friday night and disappear for a few days. When the ransom was paid, he would collect a little and the rest would settle his debts with Mickey. But when he got to the park that night, she wasn't there - just her car. Knowing nothing else to do, he went looking for Charlotte – without any luck.

Mickey and his thugs were watching from the sidelines - but when things went wrong and he couldn't find his daughter, he got scared and told Mickey the deal was off. That didn't set well with the group, and they ordered him to steal Charlotte's car and retrieve the money or he was a dead man. He said he stole the car, as instructed, made the ransom delivery call to Phillip Chaney - but then went in another direction. He has been in hiding since.

I asked him if he knew the whereabouts of his daughter – he said he did not. She had driven her car to the park, as planned, but he had not seen or spoken to her. He repeated several times that he could never harm Charlotte.

As much of an asshole as this guy was, for some reason, I believed his story. But, I was sure Leroy and the FBI would have many more questions to ask. Unfortunately, our visit was coming to an abrupt ending.

They came from every direction, and within minutes the entire park was full of police cars, fire trucks and, I think, every vehicle in Gibson County that had flashing lights. It took them only a few seconds to find us and take Travis into custody.

Leroy joined me on the swings, and I was telling him my story when someone hit me on the shoulder from behind – it was Liz.

160

"You bastard. How could you do this? I thought you were dead – and you're not! You're sitting here in the park on a swing like a 10-year-old boy! I'm going crazy and you're playing in the park? I could kill you myself!"

"Liz, calm down – I'll explain later. You did good by calling the sheriff, but did you also call all these other folks?"

"Yes, I did. I called the sheriff, I called the State Police, I called the Fire Department, I called the Game Warden, I called the City Police, I even called the Governor – but he didn't answer. I called everyone until I ran out of dimes. You satisfied?"

"Yes I am. I believe you might have saved my life – thank you."

"You're welcome…I think," she seemed confused. "Did I really save your life?"

"Yes you did, and we'll celebrate later. Okay?"

"Later? What's wrong with now?" She was visibly mad at me.

"Because I need to go to Jackson. But, if you promise to follow instructions and not ask questions, you can take me – if not, you can take me to get my car. Your choice."

Oddly, she seemed to think before answering. "I'll take you and I promise no questions. I'm afraid if I don't go with you something will happen – you might need my help again. Is that right?"

"Right, let's go, I'll buy you a drink at the Holiday Inn bar."

I parked Liz in the bar and headed straight for Phillip Chaney's room. He peaked out with the door latch in place, and then opened the door to let me in.

"Phillip, I'll keep this simple. I left you with specific instructions and you didn't follow them. In fact, it seems you went out of your way to disobey those instructions in every way possible. You can have a seat and tell me you're reasoning, or I'll see that the FBI or the sheriff provide you with overnight accommodations in a friendly jail - your choice. I've got a date waiting downstairs – so don't take long with your decision."

He sat on the couch and began to talk.

Soon after arriving in Jackson, his brother called and said he was coming over. He wasn't sure how his brother had found him, but he wasn't surprised. This is where he normally stayed, and a call to the hotel desk would have provided that information.

When his brother arrived, he shared with him the story about my involvement, and how I would get the FBI involved, and how he wasn't to do anything without calling me. He then claimed his brother, somehow, persuaded him that he shouldn't listen to me, and that they together would deliver the money and rescue Charlotte.

I held up my hand, stopping his story. "Phillip, this isn't working, so we're going to try this another way. This bullshit story of yours has holes big enough to drive a train through. This is the second time we've talked, and both times I get the impression that you really don't understand the gravity of this whole situation. So, I'm going to ask questions, and the first wrong answer I get, I leave. Understood?"

"Okay, Carson. Ask your questions."

"Tell me about your mysterious brother – and you can start with his name."

"His name is Denny Smith – we call him 'Dude'. He's actually my half-bother and several years older. Dad was married early in life and that marriage produced Dude. They divorced a couple of years before he met my mother, and then she died a few years later in an automobile accident. Dad has been trying to support him, but it hasn't been easy. Dude is pretty heavy into the drug scene and dad refuses to contribute to his bad habits. Dude lives in Olive

Branch, Mississippi – a house that dad had bought for him and his mother shortly after their divorce. We've remained in communication, but not terribly close – our circle of friends are quite different as you might imagine."

"No, I don't imagine. The more I talk with you the more I realize that I really don't know who you are. Where is your brother now?" I needed this guy to open up – he wasn't.

"I don't know. He left after we flew back from Halls."

"Is he named in your father's estate? I mean, does he get anything when your father dies?"

"I don't know, but I don't think so. You can ask father."

"I will. Now, do you know how he knew Charlotte was missing – or about your being here with instructions to deliver money?"

"No, but I don't think he did know. I mean, I think I told him. I don't think he knew anything before he got here."

I wasn't convinced. "So how did he know you were here?"

"I assume he guessed, I always stay here when I'm in Jackson."

"Okay, Phillip I'll leave now. If you talk with Denny 'Dude' Smith, you tell him I want to visit with him. You're in the hands of the FBI now, and my advice is to do exactly what they tell you – or they will put you in jail. Frankly, your stories are full of half-truth and bullshit. And if you do that with them, the consequence won't be pretty – trust me."

I left – just as pissed as when I arrived. Some 'no-good' brother shows up and changes well put together plans – why and for what reasons? I needed to think on this new wrinkle – it might be nothing, or it might be everything.

~

*W*hen I got back down to the bar, Liz had just started her fourth glass of wine. It was showing.

I took a seat at a stool next to her and smiled. "Hey good looking – you got any plans for this evening?"

"Yes, and you are not part of them. Thank you very much," her words were running together.

"But you saved my life tonight, and I thought we were going to celebrate?"

"I am celebrating – but you're not here. You're up in a hotel room, celebrating with somebody else. Are they pretty?" She was smashed!

"Yes, they were pretty – pretty revolting. But, that's a story for another day. You want to go get something to eat?"

"I want eggs – scrambled. You got any eggs?"

"No, but I have chickens. They lay eggs. Is that good enough?"

"Where are the chickens? They here?" She was looking around the bar - this was getting funny.

"No, they're in Humboldt. You want to go celebrate?"

"Celebrate what – the chickens laying eggs?"

"Yes, but we need to go now."

"Okay – but no funny stuff. I've got a real tough boyfriend. He eats eggs too."

We went to celebrate.

Tragedy

*L*iz headed back to Memphis early, so she dropped me off at Chief's in time to join the breakfast crowd.

I got a curious look from Nickie, then took a seat at the counter and ordered Ronnie's breakfast special – pancakes and sausage.

It was time for a call to Monica Jeffers. So, while waiting for breakfast, I used the outside payphone to make that call.

I gave her a brief overview, as I knew it, and strongly suggested she make herself invisible for the next several days. The best choice would be to leave town – take a short vacation and leave no contact information. Things were going to get loud and the media would be seeking any opportunity for an interview – we didn't want any interviews. She agreed, and said she would visit her daughter in New Orleans for a few days – perhaps longer. I asked her to call me with a phone number when she got settled. We said good-bye, and I went back to my breakfast.

"How was the movie?" Nickie asked after I sat down.

"It was great – an adventure story with a lot of action, but nobody died. My kind of movie."

"Carson, you are so full of shit. We all know that every emergency and police vehicle in Humboldt was called to Bailey Park last night to save your ass. And, since you're sitting here having pancakes and sausage, I see that they must have been successful."

"Are you disappointed?" I was teasing her.

"Of course not. Normally the most excitement we get around here are loose cows running down Hwy 45. But when you're in town, we get to really see our tax dollars at work. With all he police activity last night, Ronnie thought the Russians had invaded. I didn't tell him different, and it was this morning before he finally learned the truth."

"Why did you spoil the fun?"

"Because he had all his guns loaded and out on the counter – I was afraid he might shoot the first strange looking customer who walked in the door!"

"Nickie, you are precious. Did I have any calls last night?"

"Just one, but it was late. Marcie called and left a phone number – she said it was for a Forrest Chaney. He had called yesterday and asked you to return his call. It is a Memphis number; let me get it for you."

She brought me the number along with my pancakes and sausage. I debated about calling Forrest Chaney this morning – I decided to put it off until things shook themselves out a little more. I was only going to get one good chance and I wanted to have more facts before talking to him.

Breakfast finished, I was having my second cup of coffee when Leroy's cruiser pulled into the parking lot. He opened the front door, saw me and motioned me to join him.

"What's up?" I asked as I took the passenger seat in his Gibson County Sheriff's cruiser.

"Several things and they're all bad. Some fishermen found a body floating in Humboldt Lake. It's been there a few days and there's no identification – but it's reported to be a young female. You and I are headed there now."

"Oh my!" My thoughts were the worst.

"There's more. Travis is locked in my jail and singing loudly to the FBI. There's pressure on us to pick up Mickey Campbell for questioning. That's not going to set well, so you need to be aware. His guys will probably come after you."

"Okay, I'm now aware. We can discuss that later. Do you think this might be Charlotte Luckey floating in the lake?" I didn't want to ask that.

"Carson, this is getting complicated. I sure hope it isn't."

"So do I...so do I," I repeated.

Humboldt Lake

*W*e headed to Humboldt Lake at a rapid rate – lights, siren and observing no speed limit. As we rushed past 'Reg's' bait shop on the lake highway, he reminded me that it was owned by Lee and Barbara Stevens, the ex-wife of the football coach Charlotte had been involved with in Trenton.

"Really? I asked. "Where is the coach now?"

"He owns and runs a beer joint at the Gibson/Madison County Line on Hwy 45 – called 'My Place'. We've had a few calls, but nothing serious – underage drinking, fights – the usual stuff."

There were two police cars and an ambulance in the parking area when we arrived. Jeff Cole and Scotty Perry were interviewing the two fishermen, and I stood aside to observe the activities. I watched the covered body being moved from a boat to a stretcher and then placed into the waiting ambulance – it quickly left. Jeff walked over to update Leroy, and Scotty walked over to me.

"What do you know?" I asked.

"Not much. Two guys were fishing and found this floating and very bloated body. They called the office and here we are. It's a female, young and naked. Other than that, we couldn't tell much about the crime – assuming there was a crime."

"Drowned swimming?" I should not have said that.

"Look Carson. That was not a pretty sight. Dead woman, floating in the water for several days, with fish and other critters having their bites – just don't push the issue. Okay?"

"I'm sorry Scotty. Anybody see anything?"

"Not that we know of. There's no attendant and nobody is ever out here unless they're fishing. We'll check, of course, but nothing now."

Both Leroy and I had seen enough. We got back in the cruiser and headed hurriedly back toward Humboldt.

"Where we going?" I asked when we reached the highway.

"St. Mary's Hospital. Dr. Barker is the resident coroner. We've called him and he should be available when the body gets there. I want identification quickly and a cause of death when he can."

St. Mary's Hospital, Humboldt, Tenn.

If this was Charlotte, and my guess is that it was, there was some real irony. St. Mary's Hospital is located directly behind Bailey Park – not more than 500 yards from where they found

Charlotte's car on Saturday. She could now be in the basement, lying on a cold metal table in a morgue, only yards from where she was last known to be alive. A shame, an irony and a real tragedy.

I was sitting on a bench outside the hospital to avoid the congestion and the circus going on downstairs. Eventually, Deputy Scotty Perry joined me – he said he needed a smoke.

"Carson, sorry about being abrupt out at the lake. I had to help get the girl out of the boat and into the ambulance – it was upsetting. I hope you understand."

"I do understand, and no apology is necessary. That's a thankless job that nobody wants, but somebody must do. I admire you for your courage." I was serious.

As we were talking, Deputy Jeff Cole walked over and spoke to us both, "They've called Mrs. Turner - I'm not sure I want to be around when she gets here."

"They haven't made identification yet, have they?" I asked.

"No, but they've found a birthmark and a couple of moles that a parent would know about. With nobody else reported missing, I would be surprised if that isn't Charlotte Luckey," Jeff was almost in tears.

"Did you know her well?" I asked.

"Sure – everybody knew Charlotte. Scotty and I practically went to school with her – she was younger, but everybody knew or wanted to know Charlotte. This is a tragedy for our little community, and none of us will rest until we find the bastard or bastards that did this." You could hear his anger.

I saw a FBI vehicle enter the parking area and two agents exit the car and enter the building.

Scotty spoke when he saw their vehicle. "Well, I guess we can go chase speeders now, the Calvary has arrived. We'll be fetching coffee and making phone calls – the FBI doesn't cooperate or share information with anybody."

"I know – but remember my hands aren't tied like Leroy's. I don't intend to follow them around; they don't have any jurisdiction over me." I was trying to give them a different point of view.

"No Carson, when you get in their way, they'll just lock your ass up – that's all," Jeff replied.

"Maybe. But until they do, I'm freelance. Okay?"

"Let us know if we can help – we both mean that, and I'm sure Leroy does too," Scotty replied.

"Did you find anything at the lake?"

Jeff spoke. "Yes we did. The body was dropped into the lake somewhere on the southeast side – we believe. There's a dirt farm road that travels right up the lake; it's a teenage parking area – you know where kids go to park, drink and act older than they are. We never go out there – actually it's really in Crockett County, but they never hassle the kids either."

"Anything else?" I asked.

"The body was weighted with two bricks, which any idiot should know wouldn't hold it down for long. You can add that to your notes - body dumping wasn't a highlight on their resume."

"Good information." It really was.

"We also found some good tire prints. But who knows from what or when. We made some plaster molds and we'll have the finished product tomorrow after they dry. However, without some match, that tells us absolutely nothing. I'm afraid we don't have much – everybody we talked to saw nothing or know nothing. But don't forget, we now have the FBI – I'm sure they will have this solved before daylight."

"Jeff, don't get discouraged. Let me give you a suggestion. When you get those tire molds, compare them to Charlotte's T-Bird. I'm betting you will find a match. If not, you should get Memphis to check that Chrysler you ran the plates on and any other vehicle you can link to Mickey Campbell. If that doesn't work, I would check the limo service Phillip Chaney uses. I'm sure the FBI will be checking on vehicles owned by Billy Vickers, Lee Stevens and Coach James Gannon – let them do that. But I think you'll trump them with your first search."

"Wow, Carson, good idea. Have you discussed all this with Leroy?" Scotty asked.

"Not yet, but I will. I also need you to do another thing. You game?"

"Sure. What is it?" Jeff asked.

"I need you to check on a Denny 'Dude' Smith. A resident of Olive Branch, Mississippi – I think. He's the half-brother of Phillip Chaney. Leroy has met him, but I don't think he got his full story.

I have a hunch he might be staying somewhere local – a rental or a hotel. Check him out, and let me and Leroy know what you find."

Jeff spoke, "Thanks, Carson. Being busy and contributing is the best medicine for something like this. Just keep us straight with Leroy, and we'll do whatever we can to put this bastard in the electric chair."

"One more thing. According to Phillip Chaney, Charlotte called him at the Holiday Inn sometime late Friday night. I need to know what time and from where that call was made – if it really happened. Can you do that too?"

"No problem – we'll have that information tonight or tomorrow. Anything else?"

"Yes, can one of you give me a ride back to Chief's?"

I saw Loretta Turner pulling into the parking lot as Jeff and I were leaving. Like them, I was glad I would not be around for what happened next.

~

*N*ickie brought me a drink and immediately knew something was wrong.

"You okay, Mr. Detective? You seem troubled this afternoon."

"I am – but not sure for what reason." She didn't understand that reply.

"Drink up. An empty glass will absorb your troubles. I know. I run a bar – remember?"

"That's not it Nickie. You'll hear about it later, but I think they have found that beauty queen, Charlotte Luckey dead. I'm obviously upset from that, but I'm more troubled by who the killer may be."

"Tell me Carson, I'll listen," she was sincere.

"I just cannot accept the fact that a father could murder a daughter – at least not a murder like I just saw evidence of. All things will, and do, point to him. I think he's guilty of many things, but I don't think killing his daughter is one of them."

"Why do you/they/whoever think it's him?"

"They just will – trust me. It's the easy answer, but I think the wrong one."

"Okay, Carson – drink up, daylight is still here and the night hasn't started yet. Would you like something to eat?"

"No, but did you save me the paper?"

"Yep – here it is," she said handing me a well-used newspaper.

The headline read:

DISTRICT ATTORNEY SUMMONS THE GRAND JURY

The article explained that the Memphis District Attorney had summoned a grand jury to investigate charges of illegal activities in the Memphis Mayor's office and in the Memphis Police Department. It went on to explain that future charges might be forthcoming with the Shelby County Sheriff's Department and other law enforcement operations.

Side articles contained photos of the mayor, ex-mayor, police chief and Shelby County Sheriff – all had responded with 'no comment' to questions from reporters. I felt sure they were very busy 'lawyering-up' before having to speak to a grand jury.

Another related article mentioned the re-opening of the investigation into the death of Barry Lassiter, and contained his picture along with his wife, Darlene.

A story buried on the back page referred to the recent deaths of Commercial Appeal reporter, Bernie Taylor and former reporter Watson Clark. Details on both deaths were very sketchy.

I found no mention of Steve Carrollton or any of the Memphis Mafia in any of the news copy.

~

*F*rom the outside phone I called Larry Parker and actually reached him in his office. He told me basically the same things I had read, except for the fact that Federal Marshals had brought

Steve Carrollton from the Turney Center Prison back to a local jail for questioning. He also said that Bubba and Bobby had not been located, and that it would be best to extend my fishing trip until I heard something different.

Then I called Monica at the New Orleans number she had provided. I wasn't sure she had seen this on the news and certainly would not have read the Commercial Appeal. However, she and Rita had already talked, and it seemed their communications were keeping her updated. Monica would remain in New Orleans until we both decided it would be okay for her to return to Memphis.

~

*B*ack inside the restaurant I summoned Nickie over to my barstool.

She spoke first, "Look Carson, it's just too early for you to keep soaking up that Jack and Coke. Let me fix you something to eat. Okay?"

"Sure – get me one of Ronnie's burgers, well done. And tell me how I can reach your cousin? The one that runs the airport?"

"You mean Ted Blaylock? Let me call his wife and see if he's still at the airport. You could see him there, or he could stop by here. Is he a suspect too?"

"No, no, he isn't a suspect. I just need to ask him some technical questions. If he's still at the airport, I'll drive out and see him there."

Nickie made a phone call and then returned along with my burger. "He's at his hanger office. Said he would be there for another hour or so. I told him you were coming out."

"Thanks. I'll stuff this burger down and go see him."

"Carson, you should eat better – a hamburger for every meal isn't healthy," she was being motherly.

"I know. Hey, do you like canned butter beans?" I asked with a big grin.

"Huh?" Nickie frowned.

"Never mind, I'll just have a burger for now," I nodded as she walked away.

Pieces to the Puzzle

I guessed Ted Blaylock to be in his mid-40's, just about right for a World War II pilot – which he was. Slender, balding and a significant presence of intelligence in his manner and speech. Air Force Captains were a well-respected group – Ted Blaylock fit that model.

He greeted me at the hanger door. "Hello, Mr. Reno. very nice to meet you. I've heard so much about you from Nickie, I feel that I know you already."

"Please call me Carson, and it's nice of you to take the time to see me. Hopefully, Nickie has been kind with her words. We've been friends for a long time and do kid around a lot."

"She speaks very highly of you, and I'm flattered you're seeking information from me – although I have no idea how I can help. And don't be concerned about my time – this isn't exactly the busiest airport in West Tennessee," he wanted to be helpful.

"I understand you were very busy last weekend. I attended that party and noticed various aircraft coming and going most of the afternoon and evening."

"That is the busiest this airport has ever been, and probably will ever be. I think I handled about 15 aircraft over the two day period; landing fees, fuel, hanger rent – it was good for this airport. Is that what you're here to ask me about?"

"Sorta'. I'm interested in a Cessna 172 Skyhawk you handled during that weekend." I asked.

He referred to a clipboard with forms and receipts, but seemed to know most of the information without his notes. "Yes sir. Owned and flown by a Mr. Phillip Chaney of Memphis, Tennessee. Landed at 17:30 Friday evening and departed 14:45 Saturday afternoon. He purchased 80 gallons aviation fuel and paid for 24 hour outside storage and landing fees - all with cash. You need to see the receipts?"

"No, I'm mainly interested in his arrival and departure times and if he had made any special requests."

"No sir, no special requests. But he returned on the following Monday – landing at approximately 18:00. I can only estimate because I had already closed for the day. It was close to our time limit of landing without lights, I do know that."

"How does that work? I mean when you aren't here?"

"It's an honor system – really. When they land they complete forms we provide and then deposit them in a message box located in my office door. I mean, someone could land and then leave and we would never know – but I expect that rarely happens. In this case, he completed the forms, and I eventually saw him the next day - Tuesday. On that day he took off at 15:40 and returned at 16:45. He purchased fuel and departed this morning at 09:30 – again paying me in cash."

"Tell me about flight log books and how they work?"

"Pilots are required to keep log books logging hours, routes, landings etc. Most are not required to file pre-flight plans, so these books are really 'after the fact' – if you know what I mean."

"Your meaning is that pilots might just simply forget to log flights or log incorrect information?"

"When that happens it's usually intentional. Pilots want to make sure they are credited with flying time. The pilot might 'forget', but only when they have made some trip they wanted no one to know about. However, there is one thing they wouldn't forget."

"And what's that Ted?"

"To log the plane's hours. That is critical for scheduled maintenance. Any pilot who gets in a cockpit wants to know that the plane's hours are properly documented and any required or scheduled service has been performed. Not to properly record flight hours, along with take-off and landings, would just be plain stupid and unhealthy."

This was good information. "Would that log be kept with the plane?" I asked.

"Yes sir, it would."

"Ted, I need a favor. Phillip Chaney will be flying that plane back here within the next couple of days – probably tomorrow. I would like to know what kind of hours it's logged over the past several months. I'm looking for unusual trips – not the short hops, but significant distances. Can you do that?"

"I can surely try. Should I call you at Nickie's place if I get any information?"

"Yes, please do," I nodded and smiled.

We shook hands and I pointed the Ford toward Jackson. I had another visit to make before calling it a day.

'My Place' Bar and Grill

On Highway 45 at the Gibson/Madison County line I found the *'My Place' Bar and Grill* – owned and operated by former Coach James 'Jimmy' Gannon. The High School Football Coach who had been involved with Charlotte Luckey. It wasn't much to look at outside or inside.

I grabbed a stool at the bar, ordered a Budweiser and checked out the scenery. I didn't recognize anyone, so I figured I wasn't going to run afoul of any of Mickey Campbell's men. Leroy hadn't told me whether they had picked Mickey up yet, but I expected that to happen real soon.

An oversized, unshaven bartender delivered my Budweiser and I threw a dollar on the counter before saying, "I'm looking for James Gannon."

He gave me a silly look and responded, "Congratulations." Then he turned and walked off.

That was an odd response - so maybe I needed to rephrase my words.

"I said I'm looking for James Gannon," I yelled at this idiot. "Do you know where I might find him?"

He walked back to me, leaned across the bar and said, "Mister, I heard you the first time, and if I had intended to respond to your question, I would have done so," he turned and waited on another customer.

His comment told me what I wanted to know – I was talking to Coach James Gannon. Normally oversized, unshaven bartenders are not known for proper speech. This oversized and unshaven bartender had some education – although he really didn't want it to show.

The jukebox was not too loud, and I could tell from the set-up and marquee that live entertainment would be performing at *'My Place'* this evening.

I got his attention and motioned him back over. "You ready for another beer?" he asked when he walked up.

"Sure. And Coach Gannon, I would like a few minutes of your time, if possible."

"Who are you and why are you here?"

"My name is Carson Reno. I'm originally from Humboldt, but now work as a private detective in Memphis. I'm working with the Gibson County sheriff and FBI to try and locate a missing person – Miss Charlotte Luckey. You know her?"

"Oh shit." Was all he could say.

"Look, I'm here to help...if possible. You and I both know that within a few hours the police are going to walk through that door and ask you a lot of embarrassing questions. Maybe I can diffuse some of that if you talk with me first."

"I don't have anything to say, and if I did – why say it twice. They're coming whether I talk with you or not...right?" He had a point.

"Okay, Coach, let me try this a different way. They are going to ask you if you have any knowledge of her whereabouts – you save that answer for them. I want to know if you've had any recent conversation or contact with her father, Travis Luckey?"

"I threw him out of here last Saturday night. He ran up a tab with one of the waitresses, then couldn't pay his bill. They guy's a bum...Mr. whatever you said your name was. He's always been a bum. If anybody knows where Charlotte is, it would probably be him."

"The name is Carson Reno, and why do you think he would know?"

"Because Charlotte is the only person in the world that cares whether he's alive or dead – that's a fact Mr. Reno."

"Yes Coach, I've gotten that impression myself. Do you remember what time you threw him out and any idea where he might have gone?

"It was around midnight. We close at 2 and the band was getting ready for their last set. I have no idea where he went – he did get in a cab. Guess he stiffed the cab driver too."

"What cab company? You know?" I asked.

"Only got one that comes out here – Yellow Top Cab from Jackson. Now, if you don't mind, I'm busy and trying to get ready for a big evening. Come back again when you don't need to ask me about Travis Luckey."

~

I stopped back by the Sheriff's office so I could hear bad news in person and not over the phone. Leroy was still at the hospital, but both Jeff and Scotty were there. Loretta Turner had identified the body as her daughter, Charlotte Luckey. The time of death was estimated to be late Friday night/early Saturday morning and the body had been in the water since that time. Cause of death had not yet been determined, but preliminary examination indicated Charlotte has received a severe blow to her left temple – blunt force trauma – they call it.

Jeff had gotten my information on phone calls to/from Phillip Chaney's room at the Holiday Inn – there had been only four. Three inbound calls and one outbound. The first was Saturday morning at 2:12 AM. That call was placed from the payphone located at the Bailey Park pavilion. The rest were during his second stay – an outbound call to my office in Memphis, a call from Chief's (me), and a call that came in at 1:30 PM on Tuesday -- made from a payphone on Chester Street in Jackson, Tennessee.

"No other calls?" I couldn't believe this.

"None – we are sure," Jeff replied.

"That bastard Phillip Chaney is one lying son-of-a-bitch. The 2:12 Saturday call could be from Charlotte, and we already know the Tuesday call was from Travis – he admitted it. But Phillip claims he had calls from his brother –obviously that didn't happen. He lied and is still lying."

"We know. Leroy has already sent word for him to get back to Humboldt, as quickly as possible. We expect him to fly in tomorrow."

"Can you check on a cab ride by Travis Luckey last Saturday night? I'd like to know where he went."

"Sure, what are the details?" Jeff was already reaching for the phone.

"Pickup at *'My Place'* bar around midnight by Yellow Top Cab. He might have stiffed the cab driver for the fare."

Jeff was already dialing when Scotty said, "Carson, where do you come up with this stuff?"

"I'm a detective – remember," I said smiling.

Jeff hung up the phone. "They delivered him to 1803 Chester Street in Jackson – somebody at the delivery address paid the fare. Now - you don't have to ask us what's located at 1803 Chester, because we already know. That's a warehouse owned by Mickey Campbell. We know because we arrested Mickey a couple hours ago, and that's where he was when the Madison County sheriff picked him up."

"Interesting. So you got Mickey in an upstairs cell too?"

"Yep, and it is as quiet as a church up there – nobody talking to nobody!" Jeff explained.

"What about the goons – Brody and Russoti?"

"No reason or instructions to pick them up – you know something we don't?"

"No, I just don't like the thought of them running around loose with Brad Knuchols at the controls. Were you able to find any information on Denny 'Dude' Smith?" I asked.

"Not yet, but I expect to have something in the morning. He has an Olive Branch, MS residence address, but we have also picked up something from out in Three Way. Could be that rental you mentioned. I'll know tomorrow." Scotty said.

I told them both I was headed back to Chief's and to please make sure Leroy was updated when he came back to the office.

~

I made a detour and stopped by the Humboldt County Club with the intention of asking Nuddy a question about the night of the party. However, when I saw Mary Ellen, Gerald, Judy and my Memphis lawyer friend Jack Logan sitting around a table at the downstairs bar, I decided to join them. I pulled up a chair and was getting the usual hugs and handshakes. Nuddy had already delivered me a drink before we got our hellos out of the way.

"Well, Mr. Logan, what brings you to Humboldt? Seems you are now here more than I am. Can I trust you to check in with my Mom and Dad on occasion?" I jokingly said to Jack.

"Just here on business, Mr. Detective, and I understood you were in Mississippi on a fishing trip. Fish not biting?"

"Not a nibble, Mr. Logan, not a nibble. However, I do need to collectively ask you guys a question. Last Friday night at the party Charlotte Luckey came into the house and made a scene. Can anyone give me good estimate of what time that happened?"

"11:00 o'clock Carson, almost exactly," Mary Ellen answered.

"How can you be so sure?" I asked.

"Because we just had the deputies remove that redneck Billy Vickers from the property. The deputy made me sign some sort of form, and he dated and wrote down the time – it was 10:45. She stormed in no more than 15 minutes later," Mary Ellen was matter of fact with her answer.

"Perfect, that's what I needed. Can I buy you guys a drink? I've got to get back to Chief's and make a phone call."

Judy responded. "No, but you can tell us if they've found her? Is she kidnapped? Do they know anything?"

I reluctantly answered, "Charlotte Luckey is dead. As the result of murder, I suspect. What you hear and read tomorrow is basically all I know. A couple of fishermen found her floating in Humboldt Lake – evidently she had been there since the night of the party."

"OH NO!" Everyone seemed to say at once.

"Billy Vickers – he did it," Mary Ellen shouted. "He found her after she left my house and killed her. He was certainly mad enough to do it when I had him thrown out."

"Perhaps, but there is a lot more to the story than you know. So, I suggest you keep speculation to a minimum and let Leroy and the FBI do their work."

"FBI?" Jack asked. "Sounds like more than a lover's quarrel. The FBI doesn't involve itself in romance disputes – that we know for certain."

"I've said too much already – just keep our conversation among us friends. We will eventually get to the truth. Go to go now, I'll catch up with everyone later."

I left and never did ask Nuddy my question. Will plan do that next time.

~

*I*t was already dark when I got back to Chief's, and I'd had enough for one day. Tomorrow was going to be even busier.

"Nickie, what kind of steaks has Ronnie got? I'm feeling like a good meal tonight."

"I can fix you a 16oz Texas T-bone. You want that cooked medium…right?" Nickie confirmed.

"Absolutely, and add all the trimmings." I was looking forward to a real meal.

"Carson, before I start cooking, you might want to see this message I took a couple of hours ago. They wouldn't leave a phone number or name, just an address. Said they had some information regarding that girl found floating in Humboldt Lake."

"An address, but no phone and no name? Sounds fishy. What's the address?"

"Box 1755 Humboldt Lake Road. That's all they said."

I told Nickie to hold the steak I and went outside to use the phone to call the sheriff's office. Jeff answered and I told him about the strange call. Leroy was somewhere, at the hospital or FBI office, I supposed, and Scotty was on another call – fender-bender on Main Street. He promised to get someone to check it out when they could, and would call me back so I could tag alone.

Curiosity is one of my weak points. I already had plans to visit the bait shop tomorrow, and really wondered if this address was in some way connected to the bait shop or with Lee and Barbara Stevens. I told Nickie to hold the steak for an hour and I would be back.

The route to Humboldt Lake was almost the same as to Gibson Wells. You traveled through '*the Crossing*', but continued straight, on Humboldt Lake Road – rather than turning right to go to Gibson Wells. The Crossing was still alive with trucks, workers, refrigeration trucks and railcars – it was a busy time for the farmers of Gibson and surrounding counties.

I had just traveled under the last streetlight at '*the Crossing*' when I saw the Dark Blue 61 Chrysler behind me. Bad timing. I was headed off into the dark on a two-lane road – turning around was not an option and stopping was probably not a good idea. I could try to out run him, and probably would. However, he didn't seem to be closing, but rather hanging back at 3 or 4 hundred yards and content to follow me.

I needed to decide, was this a set-up or was there a real clue waiting at Box 1755, and they wanted to be there too. When I passed the bait shop, I realized the box numbers weren't going to reach 1755. I was at Box 60, just a mile from the lake and only 5 miles from Gadsden. Then they made the decision for me.

At the lake road turn off - an old white, dirty and rusty van pulled across the highway in front of me. Going too fast to stop, I did manage to make the turn up the dirt road headed to the lake. Good news is I made the turn without wrecking – bad news is this was a dead end road – it ended at the lake.

I had a good head of steam and a head start, so there was plenty of time to get stopped, parked and take cover before the Chrysler and Van got to the lake. Having been at the lake earlier in the day was an advantage – I knew the small picnic area offered some cover and no lights. Grabbing my .38, I ran there and waited in the darkness.

Oddly, the Chrysler and Van seemed in no particular hurry. They casually parked, allowing the headlights of the van to shine across the picnic area and small landing ramp. I was trapped.

Brad Knuchols stepped out of the Chrysler and spoke in a loud voice. "Reno, you were warned but didn't listen. I'm sorry about that. Although we don't know each other very well, I kinda' like you…you know a man's man kind of thing. Unfortunately now Joe and Alex are forced to teach you a lesson, one that doesn't come with homework and you only get a failing grade."

I had to make my first two shots work, because if I didn't, I wouldn't get a chance for a third. As soon as I fired they would know my position, and I knew I didn't have the firepower to shoot it out with these guys.

Gun range training paid off, and I put one bullet each through the headlights on the dirty white van. My area went dark and I re-deployed.

The small picnic table I had been using for cover came apart in small pieces as they opened fire. One automatic pistol, one high powered rifle and what sounded like a BAR - all took target at the poor picnic table. In a minute it was over, and Brad was yelling in the direction they had been shooting. "Nice shooting Mr. Reno, you're good. Thank you for not shooting me, but I bet you will if you get the chance...right?"

He was right, but I didn't intend to answer the bastard.

I could tell they were confused, but I was still trapped. Unless I intended to swim the lake, I had no escape.

The one called Russoti was having some issues with his weapon – the BAR (Browning Automatic Rifle). He walked into the Chrysler headlights to clear the magazine jam – which was his fatal mistake. My bullet caught him just below his throat from the rear – he fell onto the hood and slid to the ground. He never made another sound.

I re-deployed.

"Mr. Reno, that was not nice. Alex Russoti had a girlfriend with two small children – who will take care of them now?" Brad Knuchols yelled.

Like I really gave a shit – right?

Unless I got back to the Ford, I only had three bullets left. I had to make them count.

I couldn't see Knuchols well enough to take a shot, and I suspected Joe Brody was making some move to flank my position. I really didn't have much of a position, just some brush and small trees in front – the lake behind.

I backed about 3-4 feet out into the lake, just above waist deep, and used two bullets to take out the remaining headlights on the Chrysler. When I did, Brody fired – not out into the water; he didn't figure me being there, but at the clump of trees in front of me. I put my last bullet just underneath where I last saw the muzzle flash – I heard a body hit the ground.

"Mr. Reno, now it's dark and we're alone," Brad Knuchols laughed. "I don't think you have anymore bullets – am I right? Come up here, I promise to end this quickly."

After shooting Brody, I remained in the lake and worked my way back to the, now dark, boat landing area. Circling back through the picnic area, I eventually reached my car – which thankfully, was not blocked in by the disabled Chrysler and Van.

Figuring Knuchols would head toward Brody's body, that would give me only a few seconds to get the Ford started and leave this gunfight – fortunately it worked. He fired a desperation shot at my car, and I made as much dust as possible heading back toward the main road.

Halfway back to *'the Crossing'* I met the Calvary – Leroy and another patrol car with all lights flashing. I stopped in the middle of the road. They stopped too.

"Carson, you idiot! What are you doing? We were afraid you might have gotten yourself in trouble," Leroy was yelling at me.

"Not me, but you do need to call an ambulance. There are a couple of guys at the lake who are in need of medical attention and another one who still wants to battle."

"What!" Leroy was still yelling.

"Just be careful. Brad Knuchols is still there, but with no vehicle. Unless he swims the lake, you should be able to take him with little problem. I would, however, be prepared for a fight."

Leroy looked at Jeff and then back at me. "Okay, you better come with us," Leroy said as he got back into his cruiser.

"No sir," I protested. "I've had enough of that gunfight, and besides, I haven't eaten and have a steak waiting for me at Chief's. You can find me there. Be careful," I said getting into the Ford and driving away.

~

I took my seat at the bar and told Nickie she could have Ronnie cook that steak now – I was ready to eat

She gave me an odd look. "Are you okay or it just me? You look like you've been swimming in your clothes, and now you're sitting on my barstool getting ready to eat dinner just like everything is normal. Leroy and his crew came through here a half-hour ago like a lightning bolt looking for you. They seemed upset, but here you are, soaking wet and acting like nothing has happened."

"Nickie, I'm fine. I just need some dry clothes, and to stop by Gibson Hardware tomorrow to pick up more bullets from Gibby. Other than that, I'm okay. However, I would like a jack/coke to go with that steak...please."

She stood, silently staring at me.

~

I had already finished my steak and enjoying another Jack Daniel's and Coke when Leroy took a seat on a stool next to me at the bar. He did not look happy.

"Carson, when you are in my county, you are my responsibility. I need you to understand that. Whatever possessed you to take that ride tonight is a mystery to me. You knew there might be trouble, that's why you called the office and told Jeff about the strange message. I'm not happy with you, but I am glad you didn't get hurt."

"What's the status of the bad guys?"

"One dead, two wounded – one seriously. Evidently you took Alex Russoti's lights out and did some serious damage to the Joe Brody character. Brad Knuchols put up a short fight, but it didn't last long – he'll probably be healthy enough to sit in one of my cells tomorrow."

I spent the next hour catching Leroy up on my events of the day. He didn't have a lot to add other than that they would place formal charges against Travis tomorrow – probably for murder. They were waiting to talk with Phillip Chaney, who was scheduled to fly in tomorrow morning. His input would be crucial in whatever charges were issued.

"Leroy, I've got three things to do tomorrow. After that, I think we can plan a program to wrap this case up"

"You're kidding…right? I've got a kidnapping, I've got a dead girl, I've got ransom notes, I've got Mafia thugs shooting up my county, I've got the FBI with their nose up my ass and you just casually say – 'we'll wrap this thing up after tomorrow'? What have I missed?"

"You need a drink. Nickie, get Leroy a beer," I ordered.

Leroy was upset. "Look, I don't need a beer. I just need some answers and this city back to normal. I need to solve this crime and put the person in jail that did it. What I don't need are any more shoot-outs between a loose cannon detective and Mafia hoods."

"Listen Leroy, I just need a few more hours. Scotty and Jeff are very helpful, and I think if I can get the right information we'll resolve this thing very soon. Right now, I just need you to let me do my thing. Okay?'

"I sure hope you have the same relationship with the next sheriff. Because I'm sure I will never get reelected." I know he was kidding – I think.

~

I had a few more drinks and then got a good night's sleep. Tomorrow was going to be a busy day.

More Pieces

I grabbed a coffee to go and called Forrest Chaney from the outside payphone. He wasn't in, so I left my message with his secretary. I was returning his call and would like to meet him for lunch today – if possible. She said his calendar was free and she would give him the message when he arrived at the office. I told her I would call back in an hour to confirm our lunch appointment.

My first stop was the sheriff's office. Scotty was handling the desk and, as usual, Leroy was somewhere else. I needed to know if they had found any information on Denny Smith and a local address. They had.

Denny 'Dude' Smith, Phillip Chaney's half-brother, was renting a house on Sandersbluff Road near the town of Three Way. Even though it had an elementary school, I never considered Three Way a town. It really just represented a split in Highway 45 – a fork in the road. 45 East went through Medina and on to Milan – 45 West traveled through Humboldt.

Evidently Denny Smith had been living at this residence for several months. Since he seemingly had no visible means of income, it was assumed he was using some inheritance as a means of support. Scotty said the sheriff's office had no record of any problems with Denny Smith, or any calls to this residence. If he had been up to something, it was under the local police radar.

Leroy's cruiser pulled into the parking lot just as I was getting in my car.

"Where are you headed?" he asked.

"I'm going to visit the bait shop and then head back to Memphis for a lunch meeting. I'll be back this evening."

Leroy was shaking his head. "There is no need to visit the bait shop – I just came from there. I had to make a routine visit for the records, but Lee and Barbara Stevens had nothing to add regarding Charlotte's death. And besides, this afternoon Travis Luckey will be formally charged with the murder of Charlotte Luckey."

"Did Doctor Barker give you a cause of death?" I asked.

"Yes, she received a massive blow to the left temple – instrument unknown, but probably something like a baseball bat. Death, or at least unconsciousness, was instant - with sure death only a few minutes later. She had no water in her lungs so she was dead when thrown in the lake."

"Horrible," I said shaking my head.

"Yes it is. Jeff has gone to pick up Billy Vickers for routine questioning. Again, only a formality because Travis will be charged this afternoon."

"Leroy, I would like to talk to that young man, Billy Vickers, myself."

"Then stick around, Jeff should be back anytime now," Leroy said as he headed toward the door.

"I can't do that – I've got to get on the road."

"Well, stay away from the bait shop," Leroy said again. "There is no need for you to bother my citizens. I told you they don't know anything."

"Okay, Leroy, I'll take that under advisement. Did you hear the information Scotty has regarding Denny Smith?"

"No, not yet."

"Get him to brief you on it. I'm headed to Memphis and will call you later," I said getting into my car.

I pointed the Ford toward the bait shop. Damn, I am hardheaded.

~

Reg's Bait Shop

$\mathcal{R}$eg's bait shop is located on Humboldt Lake Road and owned by Lee and Barbara Stevens. Barbara Stevens was formerly the coach's wife – Barbara Gannon.

It was a harmless looking place; one that I had driven by many times but never really thought much about.

I grabbed a coke from the outside drink box and walked through the small door – it was a real bait shop. They had minnow tanks bubbling in one corner and several racks of assorted fishing equipment scattered throughout the store. A few grocery items were also available; I assume some of the locals used the bait shop for their staples and necessities.

An older, but attractive woman stood up from behind the small counter – I guessed this to be Barbara Stevens. "Good morning, how may we help you today?"

"How's the fishing?" Like I really cared.

"You thinking about the lake or the river?" By river she must have meant the Forked Deer River, which was nearby.

"I'm a lake man, myself," I said sounding confident. "Never been much for the river." Was I really this full of shit?

"Then I would suggest trying the crappie using minnows. They've been biting pretty good," she was honestly trying to help.

As we were having our fishing chat, I sensed someone walking up behind me. I turned to see a very large man standing only inches from my face. He was wearing a rubber apron over jeans, a denim shirt and a green John Deere hat on his head. He wasn't smiling.

"Barbara, this bastard is not interested in fishing. He's that private detective from Memphis, and is out here snooping around. Right, Mr. Las Vegas, or whatever your name is?" he growled.

"My name is Carson Reno and I'm not snooping. I just wanted to ask both of you a couple of questions – if I could."

"Bullshit!" he yelled. "If you're not snooping, then what's this crap about 'are the fish biting'? You're snooping to see if we know anything about that dead girl they pulled from the lake…right?"

"Okay, since you brought it up – what do you know?" I directed that question to them both, but this guy was dominating the conversation.

"We know just what we told Sheriff Epsee not over an hour ago, which is nothing. Barbara and I are not glad she's dead, but if anybody deserved it, she was high on the list. That girl brought nothing but sadness and hurt to anybody and everybody around her. Barbara has suffered enough because of Charlotte Luckey, and I don't intend for her death to add anymore. So, unless you want to buy some minnows, worms or fishing tackle, I suggest you get back in that turd you call a car and do your snooping somewhere else. Am I being clear?"

He was being clear.

"My apology to both of you. I would not being doing my job without having at least paid you a visit. However, you have my assurance that neither the sheriff's department nor I will bother you again. I might, however, take you up on some of that bait when this whole thing is over."

"For that, Mr. Reno, you are welcome anytime. Have a good day and goodbye," he said in a 'matter-of-fact' way.

I pointed the Ford toward Memphis and used a payphone in Brownsville to call Forrest Chaney and confirm our lunch appointment.

~

*H*is secretary answered and said that Mr. Chaney would meet me at the Luau at noon for lunch.

A popular upscale restaurant, the Luau was located at 3135 Poplar Avenue – just across from White Station High School - a perfect spot for our meeting.

~

$\mathcal{M}$r. Forrest Chaney was a professional and polished man, just as I had expected.

Our lunch lasted the better part of two hours, and I was headed back toward Humboldt by 2:00 PM. I decided to take the route through Jackson and drop by that house in Three Way – the one rented by Mr. Denny 'Dude' Smith.

Denny Smith and I had never talked, or met – I don't think. In fact, I didn't even know what he looked like. My plan was to just observe, not initiate a formal introduction – at least just yet.

~

Investigation, at least successful investigation, requires a lot of imagination. You can follow the part that doesn't fit – in this case that would be Denny Smith – which is sometimes productive. You can follow your instinct – which more times than not will get you in trouble. Or you can follow the money – which is productive 99% of the time.

I kept asking myself, why someone who owned a home in Olive Branch, Mississippi would be living in a rental house on Sandersbluff Road in this 'no town' named Three Way. Only one answer made sense – money. For some reason he was there for the money – I needed to find out what that reason was.

It wasn't long before I got my first clue.

I drove past the house, turned around and parked at the top of the hill. Since there were no cars in the driveway, I would give it an hour before heading back into Humboldt – just to see what happened.

Denny 'Dude' Smith sure knew his cars. In less than 20 minutes, he pulled into the driveway driving a 1957 Chevy Bel-Air. Damn, I liked that car.

I got my first good look at him as he walked from the car to the house – and it hit me like a board across the face. Denny 'Dude' Smith was the guy with Mickey Campbell at the Country Club the night of the party. He was the guy Nuddy didn't know.

Now it was making more sense. This piece, along with what Mr. Forrest Chaney had told me, was making this puzzle come together quickly. I just needed a couple more pieces.

*L*eroy's cruiser was parked in front of the sheriff's office. I needed to catch up on a few things and now was a good a time.

"Leroy, how did the interview go with Billy Vickers?" I asked, making myself comfortable in one of his office chairs.

"It didn't. He's skipped – whereabouts unknown. We've got the state police looking for him and his car. Hopefully they'll round him up before he does something stupid."

"I hope so too, I've got a couple of questions I like to ask him," I said rubbing my chin.

"You're no virgin there. I've got a lot of questions and the FBI probably have just as many as I do." Leroy hated to have other agencies do his work. I know he was pissed.

"Did you guys ever get a match on the plaster tire tracks at the lake?"

Jeff answered for Leroy. "Yes sir we did. You were right, it was Charlotte's car that drove down that dirt road and parked. There were other tracks that didn't match anything we could find, but her car was definitely there."

"Did you guys dust her car for prints?"

Leroy jumped back in. "Damn it Carson, you know we did. We found four sets of prints, Charlotte, Travis Luckey, Billy Vickers and another set we couldn't match – could be from anybody, and we obviously don't know when any of the prints were made. You got any ideas?"

"Maybe. Would it possible for me to go upstairs and ask Travis a question?" I asked Leroy directly.

"No it would not. Mickey Campbell is also up there, and Brad Knuchols will be there as soon as Scotty gets him here from the hospital. And when I get my hands on Billy Vickers I intend to lock him up along with everybody else. I don't know what charge, but I'll think of something. However, if you have a question, I'll bring him down later so he's alone and ask him myself. Will that work?" Leroy was playing hard ball. The Billy Vickers thing really had him on edge.

"Yes, I guess it will have to work."

"So – what question do you want me to ask Travis?"

"I want to know if Charlotte carried a baseball bat in her car for protection. A lot of girls do, and since you didn't find one in her car, maybe this could turn out to be our murder weapon."

"Well, Mr. Detective, if Travis used that baseball bat to kill Charlotte, do you think he'll tell us about it?"

"No, I don't. But if his answer is yes, she did carry a bat, and he does tell you about it – what does that tell you about Travis?"

Both Leroy and Jeff looked at each other and then back at me. Leroy spoke first, "I'm not sure, but I'm going to be interested in his answer."

"Carson, do you think I should go out to the lake and take another look? We didn't find any bat the first time, but it wouldn't hurt to try again," Jeff said.

"If the bat is the murder weapon, I don't think you'll find it there."

"Then where should we look?" Leroy asked.

"I don't know yet, but I'm working on it."

I told them both I was headed back to Chief's, and to please let me know what Travis had to say about the bat and when/if they caught up with Billy Vickers.

~

I used the payphone outside Chief's to call Larry Parker. His update was a good one. The grand jury would convene tomorrow, and both police Chief Chuck Hutchinson and Shelby County Sheriff Carlton Scruggs had been placed on administrative leave. Ex-mayor Brian Jeffers had been arrested along with his chief aide, Darlene Lassiter. They were expected to make quick bail, but were also expected to be subpoenaed by the grand jury. Current mayor Roger Thurbush had scheduled a news conference for tomorrow, and announcement of his resignation was expected.

The investigation into the death of Barry 'Butch' Lassiter had been reopened with Bubba Knight and Bobby James named as 'persons of interest' in that case and also in the mysterious death of Watson and Amy Clark. Larry also told me that Bubba and Bobby had been picked up at the horse track in Hot Springs, and were currently resting comfortably in a Shelby County jail cell.

There would certainly be more carnage when the grand jury started asking questions, but for now, I had Larry's permission to return to Memphis from my extended fishing trip. I was looking forward to doing that – I just needed to clear up this beauty queen murder first.

Next I phoned Monica with a summary of Larry's update, and told her she could also return to Memphis without fear of being hassled by the press. The grand jury might also want to talk with her, but she and I would discuss that when we both got back to town.

~

*N*ickie saw me arrive and already had a jack/coke waiting when I took my favorite stool at the bar.

"Ted Blaylock called for you," she said.

"Great, let me call him back," I started to get up.

"No, let me," she interrupted. "He said to let him know when you showed up, and he would stop by and share a drink with you."

"That's terrific, I would be proud to buy Mr. Blaylock a drink...several if he would like."

Nickie went to that impossible payphone over the jukebox and made a call. She returned quickly and said he was on his way.

I looked over the crowd in Chief's – most were regulars and here every night. As I checked their faces, I wondered how many had known Charlotte Luckey. I wondered how many knew she was dead, and better yet, how many cared? I wondered if they had any different definition of beauty – one different from everyone else. I doubted it. I also doubted that they ever gave a thought to the price some pay for that beauty. In most cases it's a failed marriage, a destroyed family or a ruined career. In Charlotte's case it was the ultimate price – her life.

~

*T*ed entered by the rear door and took the stool next to mine.

I quickly greeted him, "Mr. Blaylock, it is a please to see you again. I understand I will be allowed to buy you a drink – that would be both an honor and a pleasure."

198

"Hell, Carson, I thought I was going to buy you a drink! Why don't we just have one and work out the financing later? Okay?"

"That's a deal," I said, then turned and yelled at Nickie. "You have a customer here that requires immediate attention. Please get him whatever he enjoys."

"Carson," she snapped back. "Ted is not a customer, he's family – there is a difference."

"Oh really…so what am I?" I asked.

"Stupid, you're family too and you know it. Let me get that drink – Vodka tonic for you Ted, if I remember correctly," Nickie said heading behind the bar.

I immediately asked Ted, "I assume Phillip Chaney flew back in today. Is that what you wanted to see me about?"

"Yep. And I'm not sure how you knew it – or if you knew it – but that airplane has been traveling some serious miles over the past few months."

"Ted, I didn't know it. But, I suspected there was more than what I was seeing on the surface with Phillip Chaney. People lie for a reason, and usually that reason revolves around one of two things – women and money. In his case, maybe both. Tell me what you learned from the logs?"

"In the past 6 months that plane has made numerous short trips – which we knew. But it also has made 12 very long trips – 1800 mile round trip flights – one almost every other week."

"Could you determine the destination of these flights?" I asked.

"Not at first," Ted said while scratching his head. "I did know they were north to south and south to north. I found a fuel receipt from Lufkin, Texas – which is about 450 air miles from Memphis – a safe fuel range for that plane. For the 900 mile leg it would require at least one stop each way."

"Interesting," I frowned. "You said 900 mile leg - then you did learn the destination…right?'

"Yep, on one of the flights last month the plane developed a carburetor problem, and it required a repair – which was, of course, in the log book. Carson, this plane has been making two trips per month to an airport in Mexico – Ramiez, Mexico, to be exact. I looked at the map – it's just south and west of Brownsville, Texas."

"Ted, if I thought it wouldn't embarrass me and everyone in this bar, I'd give you a hug. That is the best piece of detective work I have seen in a long time. If you ever want to be a detective, I've got a spot for you. Excellent information!"

Nickie sensed the excitement and walked over. "Okay fellows, somebody want to let me in on what this is all about?"

"Nickie, Ted's tab is on me for the rest of this year – he's earned it," I said patting him on the back.

"Oh yeah? What did he do?" Now she was curious.

"Don't worry about it – just make sure I get the bill."

Ted and I talked for another hour about everything. He told war stories, I told detective stories, and Nickie brought drinks and just kept shaking her head.

As Ted was leaving I saw Leroy's cruiser pull into the parking lot. I thanked Ted again and told him I would catch up with him soon. He was a very nice guy.

Leroy took Ted's stool and ordered coffee. I ordered another jack/coke. Leroy said nothing.

"Leroy, when you aren't talking it tells me you have a lot to say. So let's hear it."

"Travis said Charlotte always carried a baseball bat in her car. He said, in fact, he is the one who gave her the bat and suggested she keep it in the car for protection."

"Okay, sheriff, what does that tell you?" I nodded.

"I'm not sure. It either tells me he's innocent or the bat had nothing to do with the murder – I guess."

"Did you ever pick up Billy Vickers?"

"Sure did – or rather the State Police did. I'm not sure where they found him, but they delivered him to my jail about a half-hour ago."

"Leroy, I want you to go get on your radio – call the office and have Jeff or Scotty ask Billy a question. Can you do that?"

"Sure, what's the question?"

"Have them tell Billy that they know he was in Charlotte's car the night she disappeared. And then have them ask him if the baseball bat was in the car when he was with Charlotte. He may be surprised by the question or he may not – we need to know his reaction – but depending upon how he answers, I think we may have this mystery solved."

"You're shitting me – right," Leroy frowned.

"No. Just go make the call. We'll discuss when you get an answer."

Leroy made the radio call, and then waited in his cruiser for the response. I had another Jack Daniel's and coke.

He was already talking when he walked back in the bar. "Billy Vickers admitted being in her car and he said the baseball bat was in the car too – just where it always was. Jeff said his reaction was passive – he didn't seem surprised or shocked by the question. Now tell me – what the hell does that prove?"

"Leroy, I have a few pieces that are not yet in place – but I think if I can get everybody together, we can add those few missing pieces and all go home and sleep good tomorrow night. Can we do that?"

"Who is everybody?"

"You already have Mickey, Travis, Billy Vickers and Brad Knuchols in your jail – correct?"

"Correct."

"I need Denny Smith, James Gannon, Phillip Chaney, and Ted Blaylock to join the meeting. Ted will volunteer, I've already briefed him. The others you will need to drag in – use your imagination and office power. Can you handle that?" I asked.

"What about the FBI? Agent Giltner?" he asked.

"Okay, bring him along too – good idea."

"What time tomorrow do you want to have this 'gathering'?"

"Not early – let's do 11:00 AM, I need my beauty sleep."

"What would you suggest I tell these people the meeting is about, Mr. Detective? I can't just drag people in for no reason?"

"I don't care, Mr. Sheriff. We're trying to solve a murder and these people are involved – just tell them routine questioning. They won't know it's a gathering until they get there."

"Guess I need to start looking for another job – I'll never get re-elected," Leroy was shaking his head.

"Just trust me friend. Set it up, and I'll see you at your office tomorrow at eleven."

He left still shaking his head. Leroy was my friend, I would never do anything to make him look bad – and underneath that tough shell, he knew that.

Solution

*A*s Leroy and I had discussed, all parties were assembled in the downstairs conference room of the Gibson County Sheriff's office. Some wore county provided clothing and handcuffs – some did not. This was my show – I had better make it work.

Along with our cast of characters were sheriff Epsee, deputies Jeff Cole, Scotty Perry and FBI agent Giltner. The room was full.

"I'll skip introductions and formality," I started. "You know who I am and I know most of you. You're here because we believe each of you have some knowledge and/or involvement in the disappearance and untimely death of Charlotte Luckey. We are together going to discuss that this morning. Here are the rules - I talk and you listen. Please answer when I ask you a question."

Immediately James Gannon stood up. "I have no knowledge or involvement in the death of Charlotte Luckey and resent being here. I'm leaving," he said stepping toward the door.

"No, Coach Gannon you are not leaving," I answered frankly. "These deputies will make sure you don't. Whether you did or you didn't have any knowledge or involvement will soon come out. But if it will make you feel any better, you can consider you're here because you're an asshole. Now, unless you want one of those orange suits and handcuffs, please sit down and shut up. Okay?"

He sat down.

"Okay, Travis Luckey, let's start with you," I began. "You were the goat in this whole scheme. You owed the mob and Mickey Campbell a lot of money – we don't know how much. Mickey might tell us later, but I doubt it.

To repay this debt, you, Mickey and Denny came up with a plan to fake your daughter's kidnapping and ransom $50K from Phillip Chaney. Travis, I'm not sure what low part of the earth you come from, but that's just about as low as you can get.

Anyway, with the ransom money, Mickey gets paid what he's owed and you, Travis, would get some money to continue your life – at least that's what you thought the plan was. You somehow drag Charlotte into the deal and she agrees, because she loves you – her no good father. The plan is for you and Charlotte to disappear after the Maxwell party – Mickey, or one of his thugs would collect the ransom and everybody lives happily ever after. Your meeting with Mickey at the Country Club was to confirm the arrangement and set the plan in motion. Only something goes wrong.

Your plan was to meet Charlotte at Bailey Park, and then disappear. But when you get to the park, she isn't there – just her car. You got scared and ran. The next morning you call Mickey, but he claims he doesn't know where Charlotte is either. He offers to put you up at his warehouse in Jackson, which is where you stayed until putting the gun in my ear at the drive-in movie. We know where you were because our Mr. Gannon threw you out of his club on Saturday night, and the cab driver took you to Mickey's warehouse. We also know the ransom delivery call on Tuesday was made from a pay phone just around the corner from that warehouse. Mickey threatened you and forced you to make the ransom call, they needed that in order to complete their plan. However, Charlotte was still missing and you figured you would be next. So, you stole her car, harassed me at the drive-in and ultimately ended up here in Leroy's jail charged with your daughter's murder. Did I miss anything?"

Travis said nothing - he just stared at the floor.

"Now to you, Phillip Chaney. You're being blackmailed – not by just anybody, but your own half-brother…blackmailed to protect your father. Your half-brother, Denny Smith, had threatened to kill your father if you didn't cooperate. You're paying the blackmail in small sums – $10 thousand here, $20 thousand there – but eventually your father got suspicious and wanted to know where all the money was going. That's when you started supplementing the blackmail by making drug runs to Mexico – bringing drugs back for your brother's use and, most likely, his sale for additional cash.

Then one day the stakes get higher – probably because of money Denny owed to Mickey and his crowd. We don't know that for sure, but maybe he'll tell us about that later. Regardless, the small sums weren't enough and Denny wanted more – so here comes the kidnapping plot. You bought into the scheme from the beginning – maybe believing you had no choice. Then somebody

204

has the bright idea to involve me - believing I would add some legitimacy to the madness – thinking of me as another goat, like Travis. You didn't intend on the police getting involved, but it really wouldn't matter. If the police were watching the drop, Mickey would just send Travis to get arrested. Either way, you eventually hand the money over to Denny. Charlotte shows up, Mickey forgives debts and everybody walks away happier and much richer – except Travis, of course.

So to complete the plot you, Phillip, type a ransom note and pretend some mysterious and unknown person delivered it. How long did it take to come up with that stupid plan?"

Phillip just stared at me, not showing any sign of emotion.

"And now it's your turn Mickey. Your meeting at the Humboldt County Club was just to reassure Travis that everything was going as planned, and that he and Charlotte should disappear after the party. You would collect the ransom for Travis, he would be off the hook, and life could move forward. Only that wasn't the plan at all. He thought the ransom was for $50 thousand, not $200 thousand. And he certainly didn't know that if the police got involved, he would be sacrificed by picking up the money. Either way, your plan was to keep the $200K, stiff Travis for his share and continue to keep him on your books. I'm only assuming, but you probably would have let Denny off the hook for his debts – or maybe not. I do know this whole mess started with Denny's plan, and he was involved all the way. I saw him talking to you and Brad that night at the club – so he knew exactly what was going down."

Mickey was giving me one of those 'I could kill you' looks, but he didn't speak.

"And finally to you Denny. You aren't included in the Forrest Chaney inheritance – that pissed you off and you wanted to get even. It didn't matter that Forrest had tried to do right by you. He bought you a house and even offered you a job – but you wanted the easy money. Your solution was to blackmail your brother by threatening to kill your father. It started slow - $5 thousand here, $10 thousand there, but when Phillip couldn't hide it any more, you needed another plan. You somehow get linked up with Mickey, probably trying to peddle your drugs. You rent this house on Sandersbluff Road, and then somewhere this elaborate scheme emerges to fake a kidnapping and extort $200 grand from the old man in one single trick.

But, to make this work, you needed a goat and Travis was it. He was perfect. He needed money and his daughter loved him. So, you and Mickey force him to involve Charlotte in the scheme. Mickey promises to clear his debt and give him some walking money. Travis signs up for and believes the deal is $50K – enough to resolve his problems. Nothing remains now but to execute the plan.

Unfortunately, something went terribly wrong with your plan.

That argument Phillip had with Charlotte at the County Club – it wasn't about her wanting money for her father. Somehow she had found out about the double cross and knew you were involved. When she learned the ransom would be $200 thousand – not $50 thousand, she became furious.

Then things really started to unwind.

Charlotte gets drunk, makes a couple of scenes and leaves the party. Somewhere after leaving the Maxwell home, she meets up with Billy Vickers – he'll tell us where, but that isn't important. He's not a killer, just a scorned lover. They talk, fight and eventually she leaves – probably telling him about the whole stupid plan and what she intends to do about it. Is that right Billy?"

Billy glanced at Leroy, but he doesn't speak.

"Where she does go is to see you, Denny Smith. She's drunk and she's mad. Charlotte probably beat on your door with her baseball bat, threatening to spill the beans on everybody. She didn't intend to hurt anybody; she was just carrying the bat to protect herself...right Denny? But you somehow manage to take it away and hit her with it – hard enough to crush her skull. Is that how it happened Denny? Did you really mean to kill her?"

Denny Smith was stone faced and saying nothing.

"Now, Denny you have a real problem – a dead girl and a money plan that has turned to shit. Reacting, you put her in her car, take her body to the only place you know, Humboldt Lake, and stupidly dump it – almost successfully. Then you drive her car back to Bailey Park and call your half-brother, Phillip Chaney, to come pick you up. This was the call to Phillip at 2:12 AM from Bailey Park.

Then along comes Travis, and he goes to the park – as planned. He finds the car, but no Charlotte, and doesn't know what to do. Eventually, he ends up at Mickey's warehouse in Jackson where he stayed until stealing the car and making the ransom call. He still had no idea that Charlotte was dead.

The strange part here is nobody knows anything has happened to Charlotte – other than Denny. Travis says he's out of the deal because he can't find Charlotte – but the ransom plan is still in place. Mickey forces Travis to make the ransom call and steal Charlotte's car – which he does. Travis then gets cold feet and surrenders himself to the Gibson County Sheriff and me. At this point, he still has no idea what has happed to Charlotte, much less does he know she's dead.

After the ransom delivery call, the scam continues. Denny flies with Phillip to assist with the ransom delivery, which would never be picked up – Travis had split. Phillip believed he would leave the money and one of Mickey's men would pick it up – Charlotte would reappear and he would be off the hook. Denny never told him anything different. Denny knew Charlotte was dead, but nobody else did – so everybody else was still on the same plan.

Things unravel even more when Charlotte turns up really 'missing' – she turns up dead! Mickey gets arrested and sends his goons after me – for reasons I don't understand – probably just still trying to be a bad guy. Phillip is really confused, and probably believes that her death is related to something other than their planning – Billy Vickers maybe. Denny has already gotten the money from Phillip and could care less what everyone is thinking."

Denny Smith has had enough and he finally stands up. "You're an arrogant asshole. You can't prove any of this – it's just something you made up!"

Leroy put his hand on his shoulder and told him to sit down. He did.

"Oh yes, I can prove it – otherwise I wouldn't have said it. Mr. Blaylock is here to verify 12 trips made by Phillip Chaney to Ramiez, Mexico over the past 6 months. We can assume those would have been to pick up and bring back drugs, the FBI will be able to confirm that.

Billy Vickers had a fight with Charlotte on the night of her murder. They parted mad, but parted alive. She told him she was angry because Mr. Smith and Mr. Campbell had made her father agree to a kidnapping plan – one that involved her. And now they were going to trick her and her father and leave them without any money.

That's basically the same argument she had with Phillip Chaney at the Country Club, and she intended to do something about it. Billy Vickers wanted no part of this – he hid and eventually tried to run away. But we do know from Billy that her bat was in the car that night – just like it always was.

Then she went to see you – Denny Smith. That's where the fight happened and her ultimate death – intended or not she is still dead. You placed her body in her car and drove to Humboldt Lake, where you threw it away like trash. We have tire prints from the car and we have your fingerprints in the car. Have you had reason to be in Charlotte Luckey's car before? I don't think so. And a good search of your property and the surrounding area will probably turn up Charlotte's missing baseball bat – with your prints all over it.

Phillip Chaney, the ransom note was typed on your typewriter. Travis, you've been arrested for this crime – do you even own a typewriter? I don't think so. We also have logbook entries and receipts with proof of multiple flights of your plane to Ramiez, Mexico. Phillip, do you have an explanation for that?

So, yes, I can prove everything I just said. Everybody in this room is responsible for Charlotte Luckey's death – just some are more responsible than others."

Denny's bolt for the door didn't get him far. Jeff provided the handcuffs, and then walked him upstairs to a cell.

Agent Giltner arrested Phillip Chaney and put him in his car for a ride to FBI headquarters in Jackson. He was in a lot of trouble; hopefully his father and his money would help.

Mickey Campbell, Brad Knuckols and his crew would be charged with numerous crimes – including attempted murder.

Billy Vickers and James Gannon walked away – maybe not guilty of a chargeable crime, but guilty of something much worse. They had missed an opportunity to save Charlotte's life. They had the rest of their lives to think about it.

~

I put the nose of the Ford in the wind and headed back to Memphis. For some reason the fresh air smelled better this afternoon – maybe it was just my attitude.

With plans to make the evening cocktail hour at the Starlight, I still had time to drop by my office and grab the mail.

Marcie waved and wanted to know if I had caught any fish. I told her yes, a couple of squirrel fish and a large flounder. She had that question look on her face as I walked away.

In my office, among the usual the mail I found a generous check from Monica Jeffers – which would certainly help with the rent.

Over in the corner stood a new fake rubber plant with a big red ribbon and a note attached. It was a present from Marcie. Her note promised to always keep it well watered!

Murder in Humboldt

Hardback, Paperback, Ebook and Audiobook

murder in Humboldt

A Carson Reno Mystery
by
Gerald W. Darnell

Humboldt Tennessee

The year is 1962 and this small West Tennessee town has been turned upside down by a labor strike at a manufacturing plant. A small town Sheriff and small town Police Chief have their hands full when the worst happens - one of the principal figures surrounding the labor and underworld crime issues is murdered.

While trying to not become involved, Carson Reno becomes deeply involved, and ultimately the prime suspect for the *Murder in Humboldt.*

Award Winning
Carson Reno Mystery Series

Carson Reno Mystery Series

carsonrenomysteryseries.com

Killer Among Us

Hardback, Paperback, Ebook and Audiobook

Killer
Among Us

A Carson Reno Mystery
by
Gerald W. Darnell

The witness protection program had simply not worked as promised. He and his wife had been relocated to a one horse town in West Tennessee to start their life over - on the right side of the law, this time. But things were dragging him back, and he was finding it too easy to drift into the dark side of life again.

Award Winning
Carson Reno Mystery Series

Carson Reno Mystery Series

carsonrenomysteryseries.com

HORSE TALES

It was a disaster beyond most people's comprehension

There was nothing left standing of the barn, it had burned to the ground. Among the rubble were the smoking corpses of the finest thoroughbred stallions in West Tennessee. Unnoticed was the burned remains of a the well known owner and horse breeder - shot through the heart.

Award winning
Carson Reno Mystery Series

carsonrenomysteryseries.com

the Everglades

It's 1962 and the Mafia has discovered new tricks to get their drugs from Colombia to America. Their plans are working perfectly until an unfortunate boating accident puts the FBI back on their trail. Carson's friend has a large amount of cash hidden in her luggage and this cash belongs to the Mafia - they want it back. Protecting his friend, Carson finds himself in the middle of a conspiracy that has roots in Humboldt. He also finds a murder with too many suspects.

carsonrenomysteryseries.com

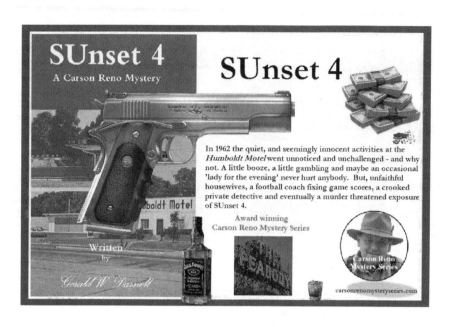

SUnset 4

In 1962 the quiet, and seemingly innocent activities at the *Humboldt Motel* went unnoticed and unchallenged - and why not. A little booze, a little gambling and maybe an occasional 'lady for the evening' never hurt anybody. But, unfaithful housewives, a football coach fixing game scores, a crooked private detective and eventually a murder threatened exposure of SUnset 4.

Award winning
Carson Reno Mystery Series

carsonrenomysteryseries.com

the
Crossing

Racial problems of 1962 have found their way to a small town in West Tennessee. A white woman has been burtally murdered, and one of Carson's childhood friends has been accused of the crime - a black man.
A town divided and the interference from outside groups brings a tense situation to its boiling point.

Award Winning
Carson Reno Mystery Series

carsonrenomysteryseries.com

the Illegals

Crime does pay - especially crime that has the support of our legal system

Power struggles, infidelity, organized crime and eventually murder all seemed to be linked the powerful lawfirm - McCabe, McCabe, Clark and Lewis. This is the story of large versus small in a little Tennessee town that has no idea of the crime and corruption that lay underneath their daily lives.

Award Winning
Carson Reno Mystery Series

carsonrenomysteryseries.com

Dead Men Don't Remember

Prominent citizens and business leaders in a small Tennessee town are dying in strange and bizarre accidents. What happens next is even more strange. Can it be that the 'last man standing' is responsible?

Award Winning
Carson Reno Mystery Series

carsonrenomysteryseries.com

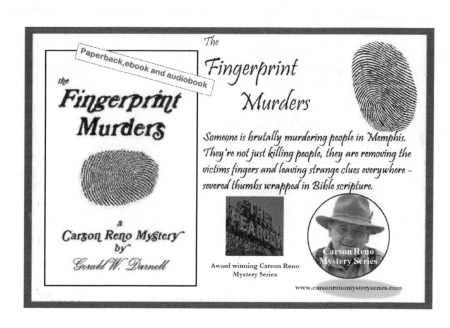

Justifiable Homicide

After a night of drinking she wakes up in a hotel room with a dead man - then things get worse! A gun found in the room was used to kill a lawyer at a local drive inn and the gun belongs to her.

Carson Reno
Mystery Series

Award winning Carson Reno
Mystery Series

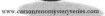

www.carsonrenomysteryseries.com

Is this the end for Carson Reno?

While trying to solve a simple missing person case, Carson finds himself in the middle of a family feud. A deadly feud with skeletons AND bodies hidden in all the family closets.

Murder, blackmail, infidelity, counterfeit money and the Mafia send Carson in search of a client that doesn't want to be found. In fact, finding the client could turn out to be the worst solution for Carson Reno and his friends.

carsonrenomysteryseries.com

216

from the **Award Winning**

Carson Reno Mystery Series

What happens when a rich client, three beautiful women, a shifty businessman, a gambler and a missing spouse are all suspected of MURDER? The results are a merry-go-round of shadows and lies in a house of cards with clues as old as Carson. Greed, blackmail, infidelity, murder, serial killers and a twenty year old crime spin a tale that is practically unbelieveable - with the truth masked behind a story that nobody wants told. This old fashion 'whodunit' takes Carson Reno and his crew on a complicated adventure, which has too many victims and too many suspects. **SHADOWS AND LIES**

'Life is cheap - make sure you buy enough'

the **Carson Reno Mystery Series**

a *Carson Reno Mystery*

Murder my Darling
from
Gerald W. Darnell

Photo Credits

www.rootsweb.ancestry.com/~tngibson/

www2.tbo.com

memphisite.com

library.uthsc.edu

elvisweek.com

terragalleria.com

harahanbridge.com

laborphotos.cornell.edu

themanhattanclubnewyork.com

scsoreserve.net

captainerniesshowboat.com

irapl.altervista.org

jmooneyham.com

gmphotostore.com

qualityinformationpublishers.com

gatesofmemphis.blogspot.com

southerneventplanners.com

chasecouriers.com

kansas.inetgiant.com

my.opera.com

ocaladailyphoto.blogspot.com

coastdaylight.com

netcarshow.com

wired.comsmh-cvhc.org

smh-cvhc.org

dfanning.com

www2.css.edu

tikiroom.com

musclecarspecs.com

Libby Lynch

About the Author

A Florida native, Gerald grew up in the small town of Humboldt, TN., where he attended high school. Following graduation from the Univ. of Tennessee, he spent time in Hopkinsville, KY, Memphis, TN and Newport, AR before moving back to Florida – where he now lives.

While living and working in Memphis, the author worked out of an office located just off the lobby of The Peabody Hotel. Many of the descriptions, events and stories about the hotel are from personal experiences.

This short story fiction work, "The Price of Beauty in Strawberry Land", is what the author calls 'Fiction for Fun'. It uses real places and real geography to spin a story that didn't happen, but should be fun for the mystery reader. As a quick read, those familiar with the 1962 geography in the novel, will travel back in time to places that will be always remembered.

This is the second story in the Carson Reno series. The first, "Murder in Humboldt", is available in paperback, hardback and electronic editions. His book, "Don't Wake Me Until It's Time to Go", is a non-fiction collection of stories, events and humorous observations from his life. Many friends and readers will find themselves in one of his adventures or stories.

Learn more about this author and his additional works at:

http://www.carsonrenomysteryseries.com

http://www.authorsden.com/geraldwdarnell

http://www.geraldwdarnell.com

And his bookstore:

http://www.lulu.com/spotlight/gwdarnell

When visiting the web-sites, you are encouraged to leave your comments and reviews of this book and his others.

Also, please let the author know if you would like to see continuing stories with Carson Reno and his cast of characters.

Email Carson at:

Carsonreno@msn.com

"Life is cheap – make sure you buy enough".

®

Carson Reno

Made in the USA
Lexington, KY
17 September 2019